Also by Cary Fagan

The Fortress of Kaspar Snit
Directed by Kaspar Snit
Ten Lessons for Kaspar Snit

Jacob Two-Two on the High Seas

The Boy in the Box
The Show To End All Shows

Mort Ziff Is Not Dead

Wolfie & Fly
Wolfie & Fly: Band on the Run

The
Collected
Works
of
Gretchen
Oyster

Cary Fagan

tundra

Tundra Books, an imprint of Penguin Random House Canada Young Readers, a Penguin Random House Company

Library and Archives Canada Cataloguing in Publication
Fagan, Cary, author
The collected works of Gretchen Oyster / Cary Fagan.
Issued in print and electronic formats.
Collected works of Gretchen Oyster.
ISBN 978-0-7352-6621-6 (hardcover).—ISBN 978-0-7352-6622-3 (EPUB)
I. Title.
PS8561.A375C65 2019 jC813'.54 C2018-905949-4
C2018-905950-8

Published simultaneously in the United States of America by Tundra Books of Northern New York, an imprint of Penguin Random House Canada Young Readers, a Penguin Random House Company

Library of Congress Control Number: 2018961233

Edited by Lynne Missen and Peter Phillips
Designed by John Martz
The artwork in this book was made from paper cutouts, old illustrations, photographs, rubber stamps, and a trusty glue-stick.
The text was set in Mercury Text and Bulletin Typewriter.

Printed and bound in China

www.penguinrandomhouse.ca

1 2 3 4 5 23 22 21 20 19

Penguin
Random House
tundra | TUNDRA BOOKS

For Rachel, Sophie, Elena, and Yoyo—
my creative bunch

Acknowledgments

Warm and fulsome thanks to Lynne Missen and Tara Walker; your support and friendship mean so much to me. Peter Phillips made many perceptive and useful comments. Thank you, John Martz, for the beautiful design. Shana Hayes cleaned up my copy. Finally, a collective hug to everyone at Tundra Books and Penguin Random House Canada.

1

The Place Where Books Go to Die

My teacher Ms. Gorham once said that a story should have an exciting opening. Like this—

We stood and watched as the entire laboratory went up in flames.

Or maybe—

If there was one thing I couldn't do, it was sit idly by while a bunch of giant insects tried to eat their way across the planet.

Unfortunately, this is not that kind of opening.

I went to the library.

I went because it was Saturday and nobody was paying me the slightest attention. Not my mother or my father or my older sister or even my little brother for that matter. And certainly not my older brother, Jackson.

That last sentence was sort of a trick. Because Jackson had run away from home. Nine months ago now. I had thought about not revealing this fact for a while, sort of keeping it up my sleeve to reveal in a more dramatic way—*ta da!*—but I hate when stories do that. Nope, my brother ran away and we didn't have the slightest idea where he was.

This should tell you a lot about why everyone was paying me no attention.

Now, back to the library.

Oh, wait. Before I tell you what happened in the library, I better introduce myself.

A lot of stories have a main character with a really memorable name. Like Scout. Or Katniss Everdeen. Or Matilda Wormwood. Me, not so much. I'm Hartley. Hartley Joshua Staples. And no, my family doesn't own the chain of Staples office supply stores. We aren't rich. We're middle-class. Or as my dad likes to say, we're *solidly* middle-class. I'm not sure why he thinks that sounds better.

You probably expect me to tell you all kinds of stuff about myself: what kind of music I stream, or problems I'm having at school, or maybe that I like some girl with long hair who sits in front of me in math class.

Can we be mature, people?

Now back to the library.

The Whirton Public Library is the size of a mobile home. That's because it *was* a mobile home, once upon a time. The original library was in the basement of the town hall, but then the basement got flooded in what I like to call the Great Downpour of 2017, and all the books got ruined, and the town decided that maybe the basement wasn't the best place for it.

The problem was that the town had no money to build a proper library out of actual bricks. This is where George Smythe comes in.

You might think that, at this advanced stage of human evolution, we would have done away with the town eccentric. Not so. In fact, our town has more than its share. George Smythe is a retired mail carrier turned inventor. He believed that it was possible for anybody to build a rocket ship that was better and cheaper than anything the Americans, Russians, or Chinese could make. So George sold off everything he owned, including his house, in order to buy parts for his rocket ship. He moved into an old mobile home on a vacant lot.

George really did build a rocket ship. It looked suspiciously like a grain silo with a ring of oil drums around the bottom of it and a nose made out of welded car doors. Now, the town councillors were all for putting our town on the map, but not so that the world could laugh at us. They held an emergency meeting to decide how they could stop George Smythe from trying to fire his rocket. But George got wind of the meeting. And that night he lit the fuse.

Yes, the Smythe Galaxy One had an actual fuse, like a firecracker.

And that's how it behaved.

Instead of going up, the nose blew off, and the most spectacular display of fireworks shot out of it.

Then it exploded.

George got knocked backward. Falling sparks caused a nearby wooden fence and a chicken coop to burn down. For a month, the town smelled like fried chicken.

The police charged George with causing a public danger or something like that, but he agreed to move in with his sister and behave himself, so they just fined him. For a while he refused to pay, but finally he agreed to give the town his mobile home since he didn't need it anymore.

You get the rest. The town moved the home beside the fire hall and turned it into the library, otherwise known as the Place Where Books Go to Die.

The town of Whirton doesn't seem to consider reading to be of much value. And so the annual budget for the library is . . . zero. Which means that all the books are donated by people who don't want them anymore. There is a big paperback romance section. A whole wall of true crime. An almost complete set of a magazine called *Funeral Service Monthly*.

Not a single book by Charles Dickens, J. K. Rowling, or Bill Shakespeare.

But it was Saturday and I had nothing better to do, so I walked over from our house. As I stepped inside, a voice called to me from the back office. The back office used to be George Smythe's bedroom.

"Ricky Stackhouse, is that you?"

"No, it's not, Mrs. Scheer."

"Because if that's Ricky Stackhouse, you have an overdue book on beekeeping."

"It's Hartley Staples."

Mrs. Scheer appeared in the office doorway, no doubt wanting to make sure that I wasn't Ricky Stackhouse pretending to be Hartley Staples. She had glasses hanging on a string around her neck, even though the world's librarians had voted to stop doing that because everyone made fun of them. Mrs. Scheer was the last holdout.

"Are you sure?" she said. "You look an awful lot like Ricky."

"He has red hair. And he's about six inches taller than me."

"Well, when you see Ricky Stackhouse, tell him that's our only book on beekeeping and we need it back."

"Sure. Do you mind if I browse around first?"

"Be my guest. Mr. Andrushko just gave us a new box of books. Do you happen to read Ukrainian?"

I said no and Mrs. Scheer shook her head, as if to say, *Just what are they teaching in our schools nowadays?* Given that the library had no budget, Mrs. Scheer was a volunteer. She used to be a dog groomer but then she developed an allergy.

She went back into the office, and I began glancing at the shelves. I moved over to teen fiction, wondering if I could find something that wasn't about a kid whose mother was dying or father was dying or girlfriend was dying or whose mother, father, or girlfriend had been turned into a zombie.

And then I saw it.

This is, finally, an exciting moment, so imagine a drumroll.

Sticking up from the pages of a book was a card. It looked like the corner of a postcard or birthday card. I pulled it out.

It *was* the size and shape of a postcard, or maybe one of those recipe cards that people used to use before it was possible to just google "tuna casserole." On the card were pictures and words that made up a kind of collage. It wasn't the original, with the pieces stuck down, but a photocopy maybe.

I scrutinized it as carefully as if it were the *Mona Lisa*. And I puzzled over the words as if they'd been written by some great poet like W. B. Yeats or Emily Dickinson. (Okay, so I've never read either of them, but at least I know their names.)

I mean, what sort of person didn't like flags? We had one flying over our middle school, two over the town hall, and another over the post office.

And oh yes, Mr. Honegger's house.

Mr. Honegger is from Switzerland. I guess he missed the place because a few years ago he put up a pole on his front lawn and hung a big Swiss flag. Every morning he comes out in his bathrobe and rubber boots to raise it, and every evening he comes out in the same outfit plus a plastic firefighter's helmet to lower it. Sometimes little kids gather to watch.

At least Mr. Honegger didn't blow anything up.

So what did the person who made this card have against

flags? And then a word came into my head. *Anti-authority.* Or maybe that's two words. But I knew what it meant. Somebody who was a rebel. Or maybe just an old-fashioned hippie.

And then I remembered one more flag. The one for the high school football team, the Whirton Warriors. It has a lion on it with a shield and a spear, which doesn't make much sense when you come down to it because didn't people used to hunt lions with spears? Last year my brother Jackson took me to see a home game. For me, a middle school kid, it was pretty exciting. The stand was full of screaming people, and the two teams were smashing into each other, and my brother and I cheered together and ate popcorn, and when the Warriors finally scored their only goal or whatever you call it, we jumped up, spilling our popcorn over the people in front of us, which made us laugh even more. And Jackson said that he was going to take me to another game this year. But he never did.

Because, you know, he ran away.

Maybe the person who made this card didn't like football.

But the person *did* like pirates. Which was a little bit funny. Maybe not if you thought about real modern pirates in the Indian Ocean or off the coast of Singapore. But funny if you thought about Captain Hook in *Peter Pan*. And Cap'n Crunch of cereal fame. And also the increasingly bad *Pirates of the Caribbean* movies.

The person who made the card was probably thinking about *those* pirates.

What else could I see? There were two letters in the left-hand corner. At first I thought it was the word *go* but then I noticed the period after each letter. Which meant that they were initials. G. O. Except small. g.o. Could they be the initials of the person who made the card?

But if so, why not capitals?

Probably for the same reason the person didn't like flags. Something about not trying to be a big shot. Also, not using capital letters was artsy. Like the poet e. e. cummings. Who I have read!

All in all a pretty interesting rectangle of cardboard, I thought. I slipped it into the back pocket of my jeans.

"Thanks, Mrs. Scheer!" I called out. "See you next time."

"You tell that Ricky Stackhouse to bring back that bee-keeping book!"

2

The Drawer

It took me about twelve minutes to walk home. Some trash had blown onto our front yard and was sticking to the bushes—newspapers and candy wrappers and a flyer or two. Before Jackson ran away, Mom or Dad would have already picked it all up, but nowadays there were a lot of things they didn't get around to. To be honest, I don't think they even noticed some things anymore. So I picked up the garbage, though I didn't like touching strange people's sticky wrappers, and put it all into the bin.

The door wasn't locked and I went into the hall. "I'm home, if anyone cares!"

Silence.

Nope, nobody did.

I went upstairs to my room, closing the door behind me. I pulled out my dresser drawer and took out the pile of *L'il Donkey* comics. They were the lamest comics on the planet, about a cute donkey and his animal friends.

L'il Donkey was always getting into trouble through some innocent misunderstanding, like eating an apple pie left on a windowsill. But I had loved them when I was little and still liked to read them when I was sick in bed.

I put the card in the drawer and then the comics on top for protection. I wanted to make sure that nothing happened to it. Why I cared is a good question, in case you are asking it. I don't have an answer. Maybe it was just so that I had something that nobody else knew about.

Once the family therapist said to me, "Do you have any secrets, Hartley? I mean about Jackson. Did he tell you something or show you something and ask you to keep it a secret? Is there something you want to share?"

But there wasn't. Jackson had never shared any secrets with me. The question had made me wonder, did other brothers share secrets? I wished that he had.

I might as well tell you about this family therapist. Some social worker from the police department had come to visit us after Jackson disappeared. "Why don't you have a badge if you work for the police?" my little brother, George, had asked her. "I bet if you asked they would give you one." The social worker thought we ought to see a therapist to help deal with Jackson running away, and so we went to see Mr. Kotzwinkle. He had an office above the drugstore on Main Street, but you could enter from the back so that everybody in town didn't know you were going to see him.

I had expected Mr. Kotzwinkle to have a long gray beard and thick glasses and a pipe stuck in his mouth. But instead he turned out to be young and wore jeans and a Ramones T-shirt. He was nice, I guess, but I didn't know what to say. In fact, I was so unsure of what to say that I talked on and on about nothing at all, something that I'm pretty good at. My mom had to politely suggest that I let someone else have a chance to speak. We went a few times, and then Mr. Kotzwinkle suggested that we take a break for a while except for Heather. He thought that my sister, Heather, should go to her own therapist, a woman who visited Whirton on Thursdays. He thought that of all of us, Heather was probably the kid most affected by Jackson running away.

Because Heather is Jackson's twin.

Not an identical twin, obviously, but still a twin. She'd had a crib beside his, and a twin stroller, and they got fed together and learned to crawl and then walk and talk together, and even I knew that they had a special connection. When Jackson ran away, Heather went kind of crazy.

She screamed and yelled and pulled her room apart and wouldn't go to school for two weeks.

So she started to see the woman therapist, and now, nine months later, she still does. And she always came home with this sort of glow, as if she'd finally met somebody who understood how deep she was. It was kind of obnoxious, actually. She'd say, "My therapist says I need to learn to like myself" and "My therapist says I have to listen to my inner voice." Mom and Dad always looked at each other and smiled. They think the therapy is good for her.

Something else about my sister. Because she was so much more affected than me and George, she got a free pass, chore-wise. She didn't have to set the table or take out the garbage or fold the laundry unless she felt like it.

She never felt like it.

Which takes us back to my getting home from the library. Dad called me down to set the table. So I set six places, even though one wouldn't be used and I would have to put it all away again. That was Heather's idea, and to be honest I found it a little creepy, but I didn't say anything.

And then Mom called the others for dinner. George came in carrying four small Space Wars action figures that he placed around his dinner plate so that they could shoot their lasers at one another while he ate.

Heather showed up with her earbuds in. I could hear the music leaking out—it sounded like an orchestra of ants. Dad didn't even ask her to take them out.

"Pretty nice weather today," I said. "Although I hear we're going to get a tornado *and* an earthquake."

"Yes, very nice," said Mom.

3

The Big One

"All right, people, settle down," said Ms. Gorham. "I've got an important announcement to make."

Let me set the stage for you. The date: second Monday in June. The place: Whirton Middle School. The *exact* place: eighth grade social studies class.

The atmosphere: near mayhem.

Just so you understand, Ms. Gorham could have run a disciplined, silent class if she had wanted to. But as she had told us on the first day, it was her belief that a certain amount of "chaos, confusion, and coincidence" made for a more creative learning environment.

I don't know how old Ms. Gorham is, but unlike a lot of teachers, she isn't a living dinosaur. She only has a couple of gray hairs, and she wears cool black-framed glasses, and she is the only teacher in school to have a tattoo. It's on her ankle, a word in Egyptian hieroglyphics, and some kids think that it means "love." But others insist it means "peace," "eagle," or even "party time!"

Today Ms. Gorham was trying to get us to be quiet. And because she often let us talk, we actually obeyed when she asked us not to. Ms. Gorham gave us her nicest smile, the one that made everybody feel good. "Ladies and gentlemen," she said, "there are only three weeks of school left this year. And that means it's time. Do you know what it's time for?"

Everyone shouted: "*The big one!*"

"That's right. The big one, more formally known as the middle school final project. I guess some of you have heard about it from the older kids."

"We've *all* heard about it!" said Ricky Stackhouse. I looked over and saw that, sure enough, he had that bee-keeping book on his desk.

"All right," Ms. Gorham said. "Then you know that every year I assign one last project to my eighth grade kids before they graduate and head off to high school. The project is important for your final grade but it's much more than that. It's a chance to explore something that really matters to you. It's a chance to *really* get into a subject. To be creative. You can choose any topic you like. The only requisite is that you should be *passionate* about it."

Gavin Luo put up his hand. "Can I do video games?"

Everyone knew that video games were all that Gavin cared about.

"You certainly can. But I don't want you to just tell us what your favorite games are or demonstrate how to play them. You need to research how they were first invented, or examine what makes people want to play them, or consider the question of whether they are a positive or negative influence on society. You need to go deep. Understand?"

"Awesome," Gavin said.

Afrand Iqbal put up her hand. "How do we actually do our presentations, Ms. Gorham? I mean, do we just get up and talk?"

"Any way you like. Sure, you can give a talk. And you can make posters or models. You can perform an experiment or create an animation on the computer. I want you to stretch here. Have some fun."

Kids started to whisper to one another. A few took out notebooks and began to write or draw. It seemed as if almost everyone already knew what they wanted to do their project on.

As for me, I started to get a stomachache.

I haven't told you about my stomachaches. I get them

when I'm nervous or anxious about something. They feel like somebody is tying my intestines into a knot and then pulling it even tighter for good measure. I'm thirteen now and I've been getting them since I was eight. Sometimes they're so bad I can hardly stand up. My parents even took me to the doctor. The doctor sent me for a bunch of tests.

There's nothing wrong with me. At least nothing physical. "It's important to understand," Dr. Kloepper intoned, "that even pain that is generated by anxiety is still real pain." He said that I'd probably grow out of them, although it seemed to me that they had gotten worse in the last few months. And I could feel one now.

Ms. Gorham was giving the class time to think about their projects. I got up from my chair, finding it hard to stand straight because of the pain.

"Ms. Gorham, I don't feel too well."

"Oh, I'm sorry to hear that," she said. "What can we do for you? Do you want to have a rest in the office for a bit?"

"I think that would be a good idea."

"All right. And if you don't feel better after a while, you should call home. I think somebody better walk with you. Zachary, can you take Hartley?"

"No," I said quickly, "that's really not necessary."

Zack Mirani didn't get up. Instead he looked down at the floor. Zack is my best friend.

Correction. Zack *used* to be my best friend.

"Okay," he said. And without looking at me, he headed for the door.

"Wait for Hartley, for goodness' sake," Ms. Gorham called.

4

Former Best Friend

So about Zack Mirani.

We'd become friends in second grade, when we were seven years old, after having a tremendous fight. The fight was over the class mouse.

The mouse was white and black and its name, voted on by the class, was Mickey. Six-year-olds aren't very original. Anyway, every year one lucky kid got to take Mickey home for the Christmas holidays. Some kids couldn't because they were going away, some kids couldn't because they had a cat, some kids couldn't get permission from their parents, and some kids—mind-boggling though it was to me—just didn't care about Mickey.

Zack and I both cared. We thought he was the cutest thing on earth, with his tiny ears and whiskers and his twitchy nose. We used to watch together while Mickey sat on his hind legs and held a pumpkin seed in his delicate little hands. We both loved to fill Mickey's water bottle and even to clean the poopy newspaper from the bottom of the cage. And both Zack and I had permission.

We got so heated about it that we started to fight. Zack took a swipe at me and, being so little, twirled himself around and fell over. I tried to kick Zack and landed on my butt. The teacher gave us a good talking-to. Then she sat us both down and held a conference like it was the United Nations trying to prevent a war between two countries. A compromise was reached. I could have Mickey for half the holiday and Zack could have him for the other half. And each of us could visit Mickey at the other person's house.

And that's what we did. And while we were at each other's houses visiting Mickey, we started to play together. We built cities out of blocks. We teeter-tottered in Zack's backyard. We made snowmen in my backyard. We ran around in circles the way little kids do, we laughed at our own jokes, we ate snacks, we ran around some more.

We became best friends.

And we stayed that way, year after year, even as we got older. We hung out together at lunch, after school, and on the weekends. We had dinner at each other's houses. Zack came with us to Niagara Falls and I went camping with Zack's family.

And then my brother Jackson ran away.

At first, Zack's family was super supportive. They knocked on doors handing out flyers. They brought over baked lasagna. And then they stopped. I was so caught up in our family drama that I didn't notice. But then I went back to school. At lunchtime Zack was nowhere to be seen. At recess he hung out with a couple of other boys and turned his back if I tried to approach. When I phoned his house, Zack's younger sister giggled and told me that Zack wasn't home. "Did I do good?" she said to somebody and hung up.

I didn't know what to think. I needed somebody to help me take a break from worrying about Jackson, to ride bikes or just watch dumb YouTube videos. I thought about asking him why when I saw him in Ms. Gorham's class, but he always ran out as soon as the bell went.

So I called his house again. Only this time I got his mom.

"Hi, Ms. Mirani. Is Zack in?"

"Is that Hartley Staples?"

"Yes, it is."

"Hi, Hartley, how are you all doing?"

"We're okay."

"That's good. Listen, Hartley. We think that this is a good time for your family to be together. *Without* outsiders around."

"Zack isn't an outsider."

"You know what I mean."

"I do?"

Ms. Mirani sighed. "All right, let me try to be clearer. Zack is a special boy. And he needs to surround himself with positive influences, especially if he's going to attend medical school."

"But we're only in eighth grade."

"You'd be surprised how quickly time goes by. You'll be applying for university in no time. Tell me, Hartley, have you ever read the self-help book *Say No to the Negative* by Ignatz J. Kupps, Ph.D.? It has sold three million copies. Professor Kupps says that in order to succeed you have to cut out all the negative influences in your life. You have to be ruthless about it. And let's face it, losing a child—"

"We didn't lose Jackson, he ran away."

"Let's not nitpick. No matter what, it's a very negative thing. Zack just can't be around that kind of energy."

"Is that what he thinks?"

"Of course he wouldn't want to hurt your feelings. But

Zachary understands the power of the positive. He even has a signed copy of the book. Don't think for a moment we don't wish you and your family the best, Hartley. You'll be foremost in our positive thoughts. Take care of yourself, you hear?"

"Maybe if I could just talk to Zack—"

Click.

I waited for them to drop by as a family, but they never did. I tried again to talk to Zack at school, but he ran—I mean, literally ran—the other way. There was Zack Mirani quickly walking past me in the hall with his eyes averted. Zack Mirani passing the soccer ball to anyone but his former best friend. Zack Mirani reading in the school library, looking up at me, and then getting up to leave.

And now here he was, leading me to the office because I had an embarrassing, shameful, stupid stomachache. He was walking too fast, so that it hurt even more as I tried to keep up. When we reached the office, he opened the door and let me pass. When I turned to say thanks, he was already walking away.

In the office, the secretaries were nice to me as always. They remembered Jackson from when he went to middle school. One of them got me a can of club soda, saying it would settle my stomach, and it did help after I embarrassed myself even more by belching loudly. They gave me a mindless job stuffing envelopes with the school newsletter to occupy my mind.

I sat on the bench, and as I worked, I tried to think of a subject for my final project. I used to be interested in all kinds of things. Two years ago I'd become obsessed with the Galapagos Islands. After that it was 1980s pop music. Most recently it was graphic novels. The Whirton Public Library didn't have any, unless you counted the Illustrated Classics version of *Moby Dick*, so my parents let me order some online. But then Jackson ran away and I didn't care about graphic novels anymore.

I stuffed the last envelope and, since I was feeling better, there wasn't much choice but to go to my next class. I ate lunch by myself while watching some girls playing field hockey and then got through history, math, and French. When the last bell rang, I went to my locker to get my backpack.

On the other side of the hall, Zack was getting his. He turned his head and caught sight of me and then started rooting around inside his locker, as if he couldn't find something. He slammed his locker shut, locked it, yelled

"Hey!" and sprinted down the hall. I watched him until he slowed down and just started walking. I guess he had caught up with his invisible friend.

I locked my own locker and headed down the hall. As I was passing Ms. Gorham's class, I heard her call out.

"Hartley? Can you come in here a minute?"

Looking in, I saw her sorting papers at her desk.

"Hi, Ms. Gorham," I said, coming up.

"How are you feeling?"

"Better, thanks."

"That's good. Be sure and tell your parents about it. I didn't have a chance to ask if you're excited about the final project."

"Oh, sure."

"Do you know your subject yet?"

"Not exactly."

She stopped shuffling her papers. "No?"

"I've been thinking about it. But these days I'm just not interested in that much."

I felt myself blushing. She knew perfectly well what I meant by "these days." I meant since my brother ran away. I knew that it was wrong to use him this way but I was doing it anyway.

I waited for Ms. Gorham to give me her understanding look and then tell me I didn't have to do the final project.

"I know it's a tough time, Hartley," she said. "I really do. But I think it would do you good to keep up with the other kids. And to concentrate on something else for a little while."

What? She wasn't letting me off the hook?

"Let's explore a little," she said. "There must be something you're interested in. What about, say, cooking?"

"I can make a peanut butter and jam sandwich. It usually comes out pretty gooey."

"Something else, then. Do you have an aquarium?"

"Sure."

"See!"

"It's down in the basement. My last fish died two years ago."

"Well, what about travel? Is there some place you'd really like to visit?"

"Maybe Brazil. That's in Germany, right?"

"Now you're pulling my leg."

"I'm not, Ms. Gorham."

Actually, I was.

"I can see that you're worried, Hartley. And that you're having trouble focusing on a subject. But that's all the more reason this project will be good for you. Why don't you think some more and we'll talk again in a couple of days?"

"Okay," I said doubtfully.

Ms. Gorham wagged a finger. "I know there's a subject just waiting for you, Hartley Staples. I know it."

5

The Excitement of Grocery Shopping

Before Jackson ran away, my parents were big on chores. Chores, they believed, could turn any selfish, lazy, or merely bored child into a hardworking, dedicated, intelligent contributor to society.

Also, it meant that *they* didn't have to do everything.

The person who had been worst at getting his chores done was Jackson. All of us grumbled, but Jackson actually refused to do a lot of his chores. Sometimes I think that Jackson ran away because he didn't like to take out the garbage.

One of mine was to walk George to school every day. Whirton Elementary and Whirton Middle School were actually in the same building, only with different entrances. I didn't mind walking George that much, unless it was a day when I didn't feel like talking, because George never shut up. Or a day when I was in a hurry, because George seemed incapable of walking fast. He had to examine every snail and ant, pat every dog, pick up stones, hop up and down—anything but just move forward in a straight line.

I picked George up at his entrance as usual and we started walking home.

"Look," he said. "I made a house out of Popsicle sticks. Isn't it great?"

He held it up for me to see. It was made log-cabin style, the sticks piled up to make walls and a roof. Glue had oozed out everywhere.

"Nice, George."

"I wish I could become really small and live inside it."

"Uh-huh."

"If I was really small, a blueberry would be like a watermelon!"

"I guess so."

"Hey," George said. "I know where Jackson is!"

This wasn't the first time George had made this claim. Once he had told me that Jackson had gone to visit Santa Claus, and another time he was going to star in the next Space Wars movie.

"Okay, where is he?"

"He's living in my little house. I can see him through the window. See?"

He held up his masterpiece for me to look in. "There he is, all right," I said. "Hi, Jackson."

George seemed very happy at the idea and began skipping, which had the advantage of getting us home faster. Heather was already there (the door was unlocked and I didn't have to use my key), but I knew better than to even try and talk to her. George went straight to the TV, since he was allowed an hour after school, and I went to my room to think about the final project.

I came up with . . . nothing.

When I heard Mom and Dad come in from work, I was glad for an excuse to go down to the kitchen. George was already having a snack of celery and peanut butter while Heather was mixing some of her gray protein powder in a glass.

"The cupboard is bare. I think it's your turn to shop, Sid," Mom said to Dad.

"I believe it's actually yours, Mona."

"I'm pretty sure you're wrong."

"Pretty sure I'm not. Tell you what," Dad said. "You go and shop while I replace all the burnt-out lightbulbs."

"You'll have to do better than that, mister."

"I'll cook dinner."

"Warmer."

"And I'll massage your feet tonight while we watch a show of your choice."

"Sold. And now, which one of you kids wants to keep me company?"

"No thank you, no thank you, no thank you," George said, and then tilted his head back to bark like a dog.

"I really would, Mom," Heather said. "But Jen is calling me in five minutes. She didn't get the part she wanted in next year's school musical and *really* needs to talk."

Mom sighed loudly and then turned to me. Mom has a lot of looks. She has a *Do you really think I'll believe that?* look. She has a *Somebody better clean up that mess in two minutes* look. And she has a *Do you want to be the best child in the world?* look.

That was the look she gave me.

"I'll go. It sounds like such a *great* time."

"That's my little man," she said, ruffling my hair.

We drove to the supermarket in our blue Subaru. When Dad drives, he often puts jazz on the radio. But Mom likes the classic rock station, so that she can sing at the top of her lungs and honk at slowpokes. I was relieved when we pulled into the supermarket parking lot.

Walking in, Mom chatted about the summer holidays and life felt almost normal. I pulled out a cart for us and pushed it forward, jumping up onto the back for a ride.

"Enough of that, hotshot," she said.

I got off and began to push it like an old man. "Ach," I groaned, "kids these days. No respect for the elderly."

Mom laughed. "That'll be me one day soon, and you better be nice."

Mom old? I had never thought of that. We went down the first aisle and I said, "Can we get some cat food and feed stray cats?"

"Now you're sounding like George."

"You want to hear George? I'll show you George," I said. And then in my best little brother voice I said, "Do you think chickpeas come from chicks? How come celery isn't pink? Can I climb that stack of toilet paper?"

"Stop it, Hartley," Mom said, laughing harder. I hadn't heard her really laugh for a long time and it sure felt good. I was trying to think up some more George-isms to say when I stopped the cart.

Because I saw it.

Another card.

It was sticking out from between two cereal boxes.

I could even see the *g.o.* in the corner. I mean, how likely was it that *two* people with the same initials were leaving cards around Whirton?

I pulled the card out and slipped it into my back pocket, careful not to bend it. The rest of the shopping felt as if we were moving in slow motion. Now in a good mood, Mom was chatting about taking up watercolor painting again, but I hardly heard what she was saying.

"Are we almost done?" I asked.

"Tell you what," she said. "Why don't you get into line with the cart while I pick up the last couple of things? I'll meet you there."

"Roger," I said, steering the cart away.

The supermarket wasn't too busy and I found a free cashier, a young man chewing an enormous wad of gum. He must have got a discount. When you think about it, gum is pretty weird. You chew and chew but you don't get any nourishment, and then finally you have to spit it out. You're actually using up energy rather than gaining any. I unloaded all our groceries and the cashier scanned and bagged them. When he finished, Mom was still nowhere to be seen. I didn't have any money to pay. I didn't even have a credit card. I'm pretty sure kids aren't allowed to have credit cards, but even if they were, my parents were not the credit-card giving types.

"Sorry," I said to the cashier. "I better go find my mom."

"No sweat," he said, unwrapping another stick of gum.

I went back to the aisles and looked between the first two. No mom. I looked down the next and the next. Nope. I got to the last aisle and there she was.

On her knees.

Weeping.

I ran up but then I stopped, not knowing what to do.

"Jackson," she sobbed. "Jackson loves . . . loves . . ."

I leaned down and put my arm around her shoulders. "I know, Mom. He loves marshmallow puff cookies. Let's take some home, okay?"

Mom couldn't speak anymore, so she just nodded.

6

Office Supplies for Fun and Profit

Mom recovered enough to come to the cashier and pay the bill. Then together we pushed the cart to the car, loaded up the trunk, and got in.

"Want me to drive?" I said.

Mom smiled gratefully. "We don't need to tell the others that I cried over a package of marshmallow puff cookies, do we?"

"You can buy my silence for a price. Three cookies."

"What is it with all this bargaining? Deal."

When we got home, George helped us unpack by making a tower out of the cans. Mom said, "Thanks, Hartley. You're always good company."

"Am I good company too?" George asked.

"You're good at being tickled, you are," Mom said and began to tickle him. George squirmed happily.

I sometimes think we treat George more like a pet than a person.

i
know
cereal
is made by
some giant, soul-crushing
corporation
but
it makes
me
feel

better

g.o.

2

I went up to my room and turned on my desk lamp. Then I pulled the card from my pocket and put it down.

True enough, I thought. Cereal made me feel better too. So did marshmallow puff cookies.

But were corporations soul-crushing? I thought of my uncle Bill, my dad's brother. He worked in the regional office of a giant oil corporation in Whirton. Yup, I thought, his soul definitely looked stepped on, if not actually crushed.

This g.o. was a deep thinker. Maybe even a philosopher.

Even if I wasn't exactly sure what a philosopher did.

I opened my dresser drawer and took out the first card from under the comics. I laid the two of them side by side.

I noticed something. Maybe you already noticed, but it took me a moment.

They both had numbers in the bottom right corner.

The first had the number 1.

The second had the number 2.

That meant that g.o. was numbering the cards. It also meant that I had both. Pretty cool. Maybe there would be more.

I didn't want them to get dirty or bent, and I wasn't

sure that they were safe enough under a bunch of comics. So I went to find Dad.

He wasn't changing lightbulbs. He was lying on the sofa reading a magazine.

"Dad, can I have an envelope?"

"Hmm, I don't know. We treat envelopes pretty carefully around here. Next thing I know you'll want a postage stamp. Who knows where that will lead. A binder? A notepad? Ballpoint pens?"

"Okay, Dad."

"Scotch tape, mechanical pencil, sticky notes?"

"Dad . . ."

"Three-hole punch? Duo-Tang?"

"Nobody uses that stuff anymore."

He sat up. "Wait a minute. You're not trying to start an office supply store, are you? Because the name *Staples* is already taken. You could call it Hartley's Office Depot. Of course, there's a lot of competition these days—"

"Never mind," I said. "I just remembered where they are."

"Will you sell computers? Because I could use a new one . . ."

Dad does like a running gag. I found an envelope in the

upstairs closet, went back into my room, and slipped the cards inside it.

I put the envelope in the drawer and the comics on top.

Then I closed the drawer.

Then I opened the drawer again, just to check.

Then I closed it again.

g.o.

She wanted her room to look like a studio. So she had
moved the low bedframe and the futon to the corner.
Then she had put the long table under the window
where it would get the most light.

The table was just an old door resting on a couple
of sawhorses left over from her father's old work. She
kept it in a style that she called "organized chaos."
Three cheap paint sets, two soup cans filled with
brushes, and a bunch of scissors and X-ACTO knives and
glue sticks lined up in a row. At the back were piles of
old magazines, books, postcards, maps, and construction
paper. The floor was splattered with dried paint. She
liked how that looked. It looked like a real artist's
loft in New York City or Paris or someplace like that.

Lately she had started to make these cards. She got
the idea after her father gave her a bunch of file
cards that he didn't need anymore because he was
putting everything on the computer. She liked their
shape, liked that they were small. She could make

pictures on them that were—what was the word? Modest.
And so she had made a collage with pictures and words,
a combination of art and poetry or something like
that. Kind of like what the Dada artists did back in
Europe after World War I—she'd seen a book about them
in the art room in her high school.

But she wasn't trying to imitate the Dada artists
or anyone else. She wanted to find her own way. She
wanted to discover what she had to say. She wasn't
going to let anyone shut her up. No matter how hard
they tried.

At least that was what she told herself. She hoped
that it was true.

8

The Mr. Successful Detective Agency

Before Jackson ran away, he left a note on the kitchen counter.

It was written in pencil on a paper napkin, and nobody noticed it at first because nobody realized he was gone. In fact, George had used it at lunchtime to wipe ketchup off his mouth. It was only the next day, after Jackson hadn't slept at home, that Dad began searching around and found the napkin in the kitchen trash.

Don't worry.

"Don't worry?" Mom had almost shrieked when Dad showed it to her. "*Don't worry?* Does he really think that two words are going to make it all right? Could he be more ridiculous? Could he be more idiotic? Could he be more stupid?"

I'd never heard Mom speak that way about any of us, and it spooked me badly. I realized later it was only because she was so scared that she said those things about him. I'm sure that she would have regretted her words if she had remembered them, but I think the emotion wiped them from her mind, along with everything else that happened that first day, because later she said that she couldn't recall a single moment.

I don't know if all families have one person who's known as the difficult one, but we sure did. Things never seemed to be easy with Jackson. He was always getting into arguments with my parents about little things. There was one week when he refused to take a bath or a shower, another when he wouldn't sit with us at the dinner table. He was erratic in his school work—that's what the teachers always wrote on his report cards. He might spend a month on one project, creating something splendid, and then not bother to finish it. He also got into fights at school, which he would start. One was about the ownership of a banana. Although he would start it, the other kid would always finish it, and Dad would have to go to school and bring Jackson home with a swollen lip, a black eye, or a chipped tooth.

And then there were the other times he tried to run away.

The first time he was eleven. A woman came to the door and said that Jackson had stolen her son's skateboard.

Jackson denied it but then Mom found it under his bed. He was told to stay in his room, but that night he climbed out his window, jumping down into the bushes and spraining his ankle. He limped the seven blocks over to his friend Dave's house. He told Dave that he had permission to sleep over.

That was the first time my parents called the police. I was eight and excited by the two police officers who came to the house. They had crackling walkie-talkies on their belts and black holsters and nightsticks. I got confused and thought that they wanted to arrest Jackson for stealing the skateboard. I thought they might put his picture on a Most Wanted poster. It was Dave's parents who finally got suspicious and drove Jackson home.

The next time, Jackson was fourteen. He was gone for three days. We didn't know why he left and for a while my mom freaked out at the idea that he might have been kidnapped. My parents called every friend and relative, and all of them came to help knock on doors and search the parks and the malls. Uncle Bill took time off work. On the third day he came home late and went down to his basement to throw a load of laundry into the machine. A figure was sleeping on the broken-down sofa. There were drops of blood on the floor, and also broken glass, because Jackson had cut his hand breaking a window to get in. Uncle Bill woke him up and took him to the hospital. He needed three stitches and a tetanus shot.

But this time was different. For one thing, Jackson wasn't found anywhere. For another, he was now sixteen years old.

"In this jurisdiction a minor is anyone younger than sixteen," said the police officer who came to the house. "Your son is old enough to decide where he wants to live. So his running away isn't a police matter anymore. We can't do anything unless he breaks the law." She leaned forward a little. "Now, if he took something from you without permission—then we could do something. Did he maybe take some money when he left?"

I saw my parents exchange looks and knew instantly that Jackson *had* taken money. I got scared, thinking that my parents would turn him in and he'd be arrested.

Dad said, "No, officer, he didn't take anything."

Since the police wouldn't help, we had to work harder to look for him ourselves. My parents sent an email out for volunteers and a small army came out. We knocked on every door for twenty blocks around. We put posters up in every store, restaurant, and on lampposts too, so that everywhere I went I saw the photograph of my smiling brother looking back at me.

My parents phoned every teen drop-in center in the country that they could find. They phoned every week. And when that didn't work, they hired a private detective. From the Mr. Successful Detective Agency.

I kid you not.

His real name, he told us, had been Arthur Sousa, but he had legally changed it. "I want people to know that I'm going to be successful as soon as they hear my name," he said. "And I'll be successful in finding your son. Trust me, I'm the best in the business."

Mr. Successful found an accountant in Philadelphia named Jackson Staples, a ninety-three-year-old nursing-home resident in Calgary named Jake Staples, and a seven-year-old baton twirler in New Orleans named Jackie Staples. But he didn't find my brother.

My parents fired Mr. Successful.

Months went by. My parents kept making phone calls, kept handing out flyers. They hired another private detective. They took unpaid leaves from work to keep searching. They missed our teacher-parent interviews. They forgot to make dinner.

They missed my birthday.

They missed my birthday because the new private detective suspected that Jackson was going under an assumed name and living at a YMCA in Montreal. My parents couldn't afford the airfare because they had taken so much time off work, so they got in the car and started driving.

"Heather, you're in charge!" Mom shouted through the open window as they drove off.

Heather, in one of the few nice things she's ever tried to do for me, bought a Betty Crocker cake mix to make me a birthday cake. It didn't come out right because she put in too much milk, or used the wrong oven temperature, or something. It came out more like cake soup. We ate it with spoons.

Jackson wasn't at a YMCA in Montreal. After they came home, my parents asked me and Heather and George to sit down in the living room for a talk.

George thought this was a good time to pretend to fall off the sofa.

"That's enough, George," Mom said. "We know how hard this has been on you kids. Maybe even harder than it is on me and Dad."

"You have no idea," Heather said.

"We want you to know that we're going to keep looking for Jackson," Dad continued. "But we also think that this family has to move on. We can't let everything fall apart. We have to have regular meals and go on regular outings and have a regular life."

"That's right," Mom said. "We need to be a family that eats together and goes out together and has a good time together."

"And that means doing something fun every weekend," Dad said.

"But what if I don't want to do something fun?" Heather asked.

Mom gave Heather her *Please don't disappoint me* look. "We mean everyone. You'll still have time to see your friends."

"I think it's a great idea," I said. I wanted to make my parents feel better.

"And I think you're the world's biggest suck-up," said Heather.

9

Leaning Bear

"Rise and shine! Up and at 'em!"

A loud knocking on my door. I buried my face in my pillow. Usually I love getting up early on Saturday morning, but the first thing I thought about on waking was that I still needed a subject for my final project. I put my pillow over my head.

"Come on, Hartley!" Dad called. "You have to set an example here."

"All right, all right," I groaned, unburying myself.

I could hear Mom knocking on another door and Heather telling her to go away. And then George stomping down the hallway singing, "We're going on a 'venture, we're going on a 'venture . . ."

Even after I got dressed and had breakfast, my parents wouldn't say where we were going. Only in the car did Mom announce that we were going to hike Leaning Bear. Leaning Bear is actually a giant rock that leans from the edge of a cliff over a lake. The trail begins down below and zigzags its way to the top. Maybe my parents hadn't told us because the hike was Jackson's favorite. He had always run up ahead of the rest of us. No matter how hard I tried, I could never keep up.

"I'm no shrink," Heather said, "but this is a weird choice for a family outing."

"We understand that," Dad said. "But there are lots of things we've been avoiding because of Jackson, and it's about time we did more of the things that we used to enjoy. Maybe it'll be like having Jackson with us in spirit."

"If you say so," she said doubtfully.

There's a small parking lot near the start of the trail. We got out, put on our backpacks with water bottles and snacks in them, and started up through the trees. In the past, I'd always gotten tired pretty quickly. But now I was older and determined to forge ahead the way Jackson would have.

After twenty minutes, my mom passed me.

After another ten minutes, my dad passed me.

A while after that, Heather passed me.

Okay, so I was still no athlete. My legs ached. My lungs ached. All I wanted to do was lie down. But I didn't complain. George did, though, and Dad carried him on his back.

When he got too tired, Mom took a turn. Even Heather carried him for a bit. Too bad there was nobody to carry me.

About three-quarters of the way up, I pulled out my water bottle again. But when I put it to my lips and tipped it back, nothing came out. It was empty. I'd drunk it too fast and now I was going to think about nothing except how thirsty I was. I might even die of dehydration!

Did I mention that I am occasionally prone to hysterics?

At last we reached the top. There was a rope fence preventing climbers from going all the way to the edge. A hundred years ago people used to go right up to the edge and some of them fell off. And then I remembered the last time we had come up. Jackson had got here first as always and had ducked under the rope to creep along the stone. When my parents arrived, they started to scream at him to come back. Jackson ignored them, going right up to the very edge to stand with his arms extended. My parents held their breath. Heather and I looked at each other in terror. And then Jackson took a careful step backward, turned, and skipped back over the rope. All he could do was talk about how amazing the view was. My parents' faces had gone white. They didn't say a word to him—it was as if they'd lost their voices.

This time none of us went beyond the rope. We stood together looking at the view, which was good enough from here as far as I was concerned. We opened our backpacks and took out the sandwiches my parents had prepared. We chewed. We talked a little.

And then we went back down.

Down was much easier, of course, but still I felt exhausted by the time we were back in the car. At home, my parents went to take a nap. Heather locked the bathroom door for an hour-long bubble bath. George went into his room to play with his plastic zoo set and his toy soldiers. He liked to have battles between the soldiers and the animals.

In the kitchen, I dumped some chocolate powder into a glass, poured in the milk, and stirred. I had nothing better to do than try to give myself a good milk moustache. When I finished, I looked in the mirror.

Yup, pretty good.

What next? On any Saturday before Jackson ran away, I would have gone over to Zack Mirani's house. We would have shot hoops in his driveway. We were both terrible, which made it fun. Or we'd have sat in his backyard eating popcorn and talking about whether aliens existed and other interesting things. Then we would have ridden our bikes over to my house and gone into my room to play the ukulele and bongo drums while singing words that we made up on the spot. And when we had enough of that, Zack would have told me stories about Camp Birch Bark, where he went for two weeks every August. Zack waited all year for those two weeks. He wanted me to ask my parents if I could go too.

But I wasn't going to go to Zack's house. I hoped that he didn't have a good time at Camp Birch Bark this year. I hoped that he had a rotten time.

I went outside. It was late afternoon and the light was growing softer. I started to walk down the sidewalk, even though I didn't have anywhere to go.

I passed a man in a hat reading the newspaper on a bench.

I passed a woman with two kids waiting at a bus stop.

This might, I thought, turn out to be the most boring Saturday afternoon of my entire life.

And then I saw it. The card.

I didn't just see the card. I also saw the person who made the card. I saw g.o.!

At least, I saw a girl stop her skateboard, reach into her courier bag, and take out a card. It sure looked like a card. She wedged it between the trunk and a branch of a maple tree. Then she dropped her board and took off down the slope.

I guessed that she was older than me by a year or two. Short blue (yes, blue) hair with bangs. Chinese heritage maybe, I wasn't sure. Round wire-framed glasses. Plaid shirt, army shorts, sneakers.

I did something weird. I ran after her.

Even as I ran, I snatched the card out of the tree. Then I kept going, down the slope and turning right at the intersection the way she had. I was already winded but I ran to the next block.

There she was, looking into her backpack.

"Hey!" I shouted.

She turned to look at me. Then she took off again. I ran a couple more steps but it was useless, so I gave up.

I stood there, trying to catch my breath. I patted the card in my pocket and started to walk home.

She was a scrounger by nature, somebody who liked to poke around in junk stores, recycling bins, garage sales. But this time she couldn't believe her luck.

A book. A medical clinic had left it in a box by the curb along with a bunch of junky old magazines. It was called **A History of Anatomical Reference Drawings** and in it were dozens and dozens of illustrations. Skeletons. Organs. The circulatory system. Most of them were engravings. She wasn't exactly sure what engravings were, only that they were made up of really fine lines and they looked old.

She slipped the book into her backpack, pushed the blue bangs from her forehead, and pushed off on her skateboard. It was a good twenty blocks to home, but when she was on her board, she never cared how far she had to go. She wasn't interested in skateboard tricks. For her, a board was pure transportation.

Her house was a bungalow in a row of identical little houses, but hers was easy to spot because of the yellow door. She had painted the door herself, hadn't even asked her father for permission. But that was how they ran things since the accident, more like roommates than father and daughter. She flipped up her board, caught it, and went inside.

As always, the curtains were drawn. The cat lay on the back of the old sofa, staring at her with only his striped tail moving.

"What's up, Tiger?"

She knew better than to pet him. Tiger was a rescued stray and wary of people. That makes two of us, she thought.

"Dad?"

No answer, which meant that he was working in the basement. She went into the kitchen, grabbed a chocolate chip cookie from the jar (the cheap kind, with hardly any chips), and opened the basement door. She turned her head to listen.

"... that's right, ma'am, for only twenty-five dollars a month our alarm company will be on call to protect you and your loved ones ..."

Yesterday it was insurance and the day before, magazine subscriptions. Her father jokingly called himself a "self-employed communications specialist," but he was really a call-service operator. The difference was that the company let him work from home. He sat down there at a desk with a headset on, talking up strangers for eight or ten hours a day. She thought it would drive her crazy, but her dad was a lot happier now than during the year when he'd been unemployed.

She went back into the kitchen, running her hands along the oak cupboards. Her dad had built them himself, back when he was still a carpenter. And then on his last job a load of wood had come down on him, injuring his spine. Now he used a wheelchair. To get into the basement, he had to wheel himself to the backyard and go down the ramp built by some of his old house-building friends.

For a person in a wheelchair, she thought, whose wife had ditched him and left him the kid, he was a pretty cheerful guy.

She went down the hall, past the bathroom, her dad's bedroom, to her own.

Then she pulled out the book from her backpack and sat down at the long table. It always felt good to be here. It felt like she had some control over her life.

She opened the book to the picture she already knew she wanted to use.

A human brain.

With her good pair of scissors, she carefully cut it out. Some people thought that cutting up books was a sacrilege, but to her it was material for her own self-expression.

For this one she decided on a black background and pulled out a sheet of construction paper. She used a metal ruler and a knife to cut it the same size as the card, then stuck it down with a glue stick. The brain went on top of that.

Not quite right. It looked like the brain was floating in space. She wanted it to look safe, like an egg in a nest or a baby in a crib. Flowers. That's what she needed.

She considered finding some old images but chose to make them herself. She used that nice wrapping paper she had saved for the grass and construction paper for the flowers. She made tulips, her dad's favorite, and pasted them around the brain.

Better.

Now for the words. She sort of knew what she wanted to

say—it had come to her as soon as she had seen the picture of the brain. That was how art worked for her; she would see something and an idea would spark in her head.

Against the short wall of her room was a beat-up metal desk with a giant battleship-gray IBM Selectric typewriter on it. It weighed about a hundred pounds, or felt like it. The typewriter had been used for years and years in a dentist's office, one of the last places that her dad had renovated. They were getting rid of it and he asked if he could take it for her. Then he left it on her table with a big red bow on it. That was her dad, always thinking about her. And of course she, who liked old things that other people thought were useless, had instantly fallen for the clunky machine.

She rolled in a sheet of paper. Turned it on. A reassuring hum began. She started to type.

today i sneezed

When she finished, she pulled out the sheet and took it back to the worktable to cut out the words with the scissors. She laid them out on the card, taking a step back to see how they looked before shifting them a little. Then came the glue stick.

One last thing. She rubber-stamped her initials and the number of the card, cut them out, and stuck them down.

"Gretch?"

Her father was calling. Quickly she slipped the card into a folder and put the folder in her backpack. When she found him, her father had just wheeled around the house and back in through the front door. He had to use the back door to get in and out of the basement because the stairs inside the house were too steep for a ramp.

Even though he worked at home he wore an ironed shirt and a tie. His hair was a little long but neat and his cute-but-dopey moustache was trimmed.

He smiled at her. "Let's have a special dinner tonight."

"Are we celebrating something?"

"Well, let me see. You're here on a Saturday. I'll make chicken wings."

"I've gone vegan, remember?"

"Oh, right. We'll have raw carrots."

"Very funny. I'll make us a stir-fry. But I've got something to do first. Be back in an hour."

"Okay, Gretch. But keep on the sidewalk. No skateboarding on the road."

"Sorry!" she said, tapping his shoulder as she went past him and out the door. "Can't hear you!"

The copy shop was only three blocks away, on the other side of the wide street that separated them from the main part of Whirton. It was in a small building between a variety store and a Laundromat. The guy behind the counter knew her by now but he still didn't say hello.

"Can I use the color copier?"

"I'm supposed to operate that one for you."

"I used it myself last time."

"Fine. Just don't break it."

"Do my best."

She went to the shelves of paper and counted out fifteen rectangles of thick cardstock. Fifteen was all she could afford. She put them in the machine's paper tray and then took out the card and placed it face down on the glass. The machine spat out the copies and she took them over to a small table to cut them out with a ruler and knife.

"How many?" asked the guy, reluctantly looking away from his phone. She gave him a twenty-dollar bill and he gave her back change. Then she stacked up the fifteen cards and put them in the pocket of her hoodie.

Her first stop was the Laundromat next door. Inside there was a shelf where people left flyers for dog walking and yoga classes. She pulled a card out of her pocket and put it on the shelf.

Outside again, she skated a couple of blocks before leaving another card on top of a newspaper box.

She put one between the slats of a fence.

Another tucked partway behind a community meeting poster on a telephone pole.

One on a bike rack.

Would anybody find them? And if they did, would they bother to look at them? Or would they use them to pick their teeth, fold their chewing gum into, or just toss into the trash? Maybe they'd get knocked to the ground and stepped on over and over.

But maybe a few people, or even just one person would look at her card. Maybe that one person was having a crummy day, or was worried about something, and would look at the card and have a little moment of enjoyment. Maybe the person would look at the words and understand them or think they were nonsense, but they would think and feel something.

At least she hoped so.

She could see her own high school now. She didn't like school, or anyone who went there, and didn't really want some kid she knew to find one. So she stopped where she was and pulled out a card and reached up to wedge it into the branches of a tree.

Well, that was done.

She turned and saw a kid down the block. Staring at her. She didn't like being stared at, even if she did have blue hair, and she jumped onto her skateboard and went back down the sloping street, turning at the corner. She stopped again to properly put on her backpack, which she had thrown onto one shoulder.

"Hey!"

It was that kid. Why was he calling to her? Was he following her? Her instinct was to get away so she pushed off on her board and didn't look back.

11

The Metal Box

I walked back home, the card safe in my back pocket. Mom and Dad were still napping, Heather was turning into a prune in the tub, and George was in his room talking to himself as the soldiers and the animals did battle.

"Take that, giraffe, you long-necked freak!"

"And you're a hairless human dork! I'm going to send in the zebras!"

I went into my room, turned on the desk lamp, and lay down the card.

I did just as the card told me to. I thought about my brain.

It creeped me out.

I had to shake myself to get rid of the feeling. Then I looked at the card again. It wasn't exactly like the others. No evil corporations or anything like that. It was just about being alive. It was saying, *Try this, fellow human.*

Pretty cool, actually.

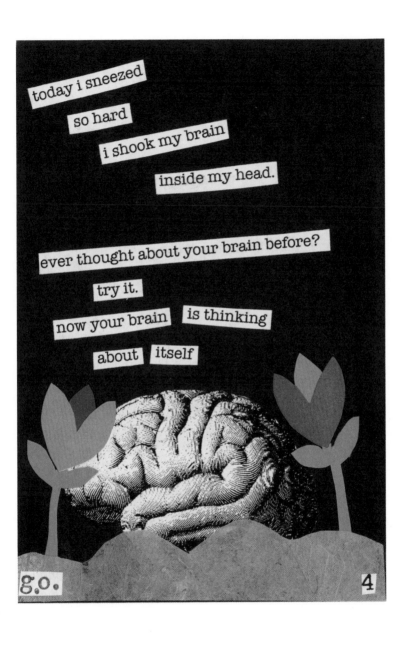

today i sneezed

so hard

i shook my brain

inside my head.

ever thought about your brain before?

try it.

now your brain   is thinking

about   itself

g.o.   4

And then I thought about my brain thinking it was cool, and then thinking that it was thinking it was cool, and I got creeped out all over again.

I was about to put the card away when I decided that an envelope wasn't safe enough. I needed something solid. So I went down to the basement—a *finished* basement, as my parents always said with pride, as if it were equivalent to the basement of the Taj Mahal. I went past the Ping-Pong table and some plastic containers of winter clothes and old toys to a wall of shelves. The shelves were crammed with all kinds of junk. And somewhere in that junk was—

Found it.

A metal recipe box.

I opened the hinged top. There was nothing inside except a dead spider and a penny. Back in my room, I wiped it out with a T-shirt and put all three cards into it. Then I closed the top.

Nice.

I opened it again, took out the cards, and laid them on the bed. And noticed something.

"Oh no!"

I guess I said it out loud, because my sister answered from the hallway.

"What's wrong, Hartley? Just realized how dumb you are?"

"That's some razor wit you've got, sis."

I waited for the sound of her door to close. Then I looked at the cards again. The new card had a number 4 on it. That meant I had 1, 2, and 4.

I was missing number 3.

I didn't know why it bugged me so much that I was missing one, but it did. I needed to find that card.

12

Get Out of Jail Free

On Monday, Ms. Gorham gave us thirty minutes to work on our final projects.

Simon Asch opened a book about the history of baseball.

Lauren Engerer took out a file of dog pictures cut from magazines.

Ricky Stackhouse took out his overdue book on beekeeping as well as a pile of pamphlets from the Department of Agriculture.

My former best friend, Zack Mirani, opened . . . I don't know what he opened because I made sure not to look. Even a rejected friend has to have some self-respect.

And me? I opened a notebook to an empty page.

I picked up a pencil.

I tapped it on the notebook.

I wrote, *Final Project Ideas.*

I stared at the page. I looked up at the clock. Three minutes went by.

Seven minutes.

A shadow fell over my desk. Looking up, I saw Ms. Gorham frowning at me.

"I think you better come and see me again after school, Hartley."

And so, once more I went to Ms. Gorham's class after the last bell. She was erasing the board and when she turned around she had a chalk smudge on her cheek. It seemed awkward to mention it, so I didn't.

Ms. Gorham smiled. "Hartley. How nice of you to come."

"You asked me to, Ms. Gorham."

"I'm being polite, Hartley. Sit down. It looks to me like you're still having some trouble coming up with a topic for your final project. I have to say, this problem has never happened in my class before. Not in twelve years of teaching."

"It's just that I don't want to choose a topic that I'll regret, maybe for the rest of my life. It's a big decision."

"It's not *that* big. Maybe I can help. How about I prompt you with some more questions?"

"Okay."

"Good. What do you want to do when you grow up?"

"Get a job, I guess."

"But what sort of job?"

"A high-paying one?"

"Okay, then. What does your father do?"

"He works at the town hall."

"How interesting. What are his responsibilities?"

"Well, if a garbage can in the park gets knocked over, he sends a crew to clean it up. Or if there's a leak in the roof over the Saturday vegetable market, he gets it fixed. Well, he doesn't actually get it fixed. He tells the person who tells another person to get it fixed."

"I see. And your mother?"

"She's an accountant for Old-Time Country Furniture. There are three stores in different towns so she has to add up a lot of numbers."

"Furniture, huh? How about doing your final project on rocking chairs?"

"Have you ever been in a rocking chair, Ms. Gorham? That movement makes me nauseous."

"Let's try another tack. Are you interested in animals?"

"You mean wild animals?"

"Could be."

"I'm afraid of wolves. Also snakes. I'm a little bit afraid of skunks and really afraid of sharks. Is a squirrel a wild animal? Most people like squirrels, but when I was little, a squirrel threw a peanut at me."

Ms. Gorham sighed. "Let's say, Hartley, I were to leave you alone in this room for ten minutes. What would you think about?"

I knew what I would think about. I'd think about g.o. and the cards she made. I'd wonder why she made them and if she would make more and where card number 3 was. But for some reason, I didn't want to tell Ms. Gorham about the cards.

"I guess I'd be wondering what you were doing for those ten minutes," I said.

Ms. Gorham nodded her head. "I understand," she said. "You don't want to tell me the truth."

"I don't?"

"You don't want to tell me that you'd be thinking about your brother, Jackson. But I understand. I had thought that doing the project would be a good way for you to think about something else. But maybe it's too big a challenge for you right now. I'm going to give you an exemption, Hartley. You don't have to do the project."

I stared at Ms. Gorham. This was exactly what I had wanted in the first place, a get-out-of-jail-free card, a pass that would allow me to skip the final project and still graduate so that I could go to high school next year.

Why, then, did the thought of it suddenly make me feel awful?

Maybe I didn't want to be different from the other kids. Maybe I didn't want to believe I wasn't capable of doing it. Maybe I just didn't want to use Jackson's running away for my own advantage.

"I really appreciate that, Ms. Gorham," I said. "But I don't think an exemption would be fair to the other kids in the class. And you were right, it would be good for me to do the final project. I'll think of something."

Ms. Gorham looked across the desk at me and her eyes filled with tears. She reached out and put her hand on mine.

"You're really something, Hartley Staples. I'm honored to know you."

A tear ran through the chalk smudge on her cheek. I waited until she took her hand away and then I got up and left the classroom. I was so shocked by Ms. Gorham crying that I forgot to pick up George. I had to turn around again.

I was really something, all right.

13

Hello, Cheese

Our walk home from school was even slower than usual. It had become windy, but it wasn't the wind holding us back. George had learned about four-leaf clovers from another kid and insisted on searching every patch of grass to find one. I finally had to find a three-leaf clover and then split one of the tiny leaves in half to make it look like a four-leaf. Then I had to steer George toward it.

"I found one, I found one!" George sang. He held it up and danced around. "I wish for a pet elephant! I wish that I had rocket boosters on my feet! I wish that when I burped a diamond came up!"

The wind blew the clover out of his hand. "Ahh!" George cried, chasing after it. But the clover was gone.

George walked with his head down, as if he had just lost a million dollars on the stock market. But he was quiet, and I got to think about g.o. It wasn't as if she was some great artist. (Were the cards even art?) Or a great poet.

(Were the words poetry?) Or a great philosopher either. She was just a teenager with blue hair making weird little cards that probably nobody cared about.

Nobody but me, anyway. Maybe I envied g.o. because she had something she liked doing. That she felt passionate about, to use Ms. Gorham's word. I bet g.o. hadn't had trouble coming up with her final project when she was in eighth grade.

At last we reached our front door. Mom was working from home today and put out a snack of carrot sticks and squares of cheddar cheese. Snacks always cheered up George. He began to make his food talk.

"Hello, carrot."

"Hello, cheese."

"Hey, we're both orange! Let's get married!"

It wasn't exactly Shakespeare, but Mom and I laughed. I turned my head to watch some leaves blowing past the kitchen window.

"That wind blew all my laundry off the line," Mom said.

More leaves flew by.

A couple of birds.

A card.

Yes, a card! I was sure of it. Doing somersaults in the air.

I pushed back my chair and ran. "Back in a sec!"

"Can I eat your cheese?" George asked.

"Don't go outside without your shoes," Mom called.

But I didn't have time for shoes. I threw open the front door and ran out in my socks. The wind was stronger now, making the leaves rattle on the trees. I looked up and down but I didn't see any card.

A plastic shopping bag rose up into the sky. I followed it with my eyes as it made a loop the loop and then came twisting down to the road. It skidded along until it was caught against the curb.

And there was the card beside it!

Leaping, I landed on a stone and yelped. I had to hop the rest of the way but I got to the curb and snatched up the card. I hurried back into the house.

"You're going to have to learn to darn your own socks," Mom called from the kitchen.

Heather was just coming down the stairs. "Nobody darns socks anymore," she said. "Not even nerds like Hartley."

I rushed past her to get to my own room. Closed the door. Went to the desk. Turned on the light. Put down the card.

I thought that the dog looked friendly. A lot more friendly than the Doberman pinscher that lived down the

today
i met
a dog
in the park.

he looked up
at me
with his
brown eyes.

i think
maybe
he understood
me

g.o.

5

street and always chased me on my bike. Maybe the dog on the card would understand me too.

Maybe he'd understand why I couldn't come up with a topic for my final project.

This one was number 5, so I hadn't missed another one. Now I took out the metal box and laid all the cards on the desk.

It was like having my own little art gallery.

I put them back in the box and put the box in the drawer.

It felt good to have found another one, really good. But I still wanted to know something about g.o. I knew she was a teenage girl who lived around here. That meant she went to high school. The same high school as my sister, Heather.

Maybe Heather knew who g.o. was.

14

The Room

The idea of my sister helping *me* was enough to send me into a fit of bitter laughter.

This is me, laughing bitterly.

Now Jackson was different. If you said, "Hey, Jackson, can you help me pick this extremely heavy sofa up over my head for no reason?" Jackson would answer, "Sure, man," and run over. The problem occurred when you asked Jackson to do something in a day or two. Because he never remembered. With him it was out of sight, out of mind. Sometimes I thought that he forgot he even had a brother named Hartley. If he passed me somewhere outside the house, like on the sidewalk in front of school, he would look at me as if he'd never seen me before. If I said, "Hi, Jackson," he would nod and give me a half smile, at the same time squinting his eyes as if trying to figure out where he might have met me.

Heather certainly never forgot me. That is, she never forgot to insult me. "You actually think that's funny?" she would say if I laughed at the television. She said my hand-writing looked like "mouse diarrhea." She barked, "Get out of my chair," no matter where I was sitting. And when she couldn't think of anything in particular, she just said, "You have a revolting personality."

All these insults should have killed any desire to actually be friends with her. They would have if I were a normal person. But I guess that I'm not because they didn't. Last month I found a pile of free music magazines that somebody had left in a box. I took the one with Heather's favorite band on the cover and left it by her door. The magazine was gone an hour later, but I never got a thank-you from her.

A couple of weeks ago, I bought a package of black licorice. Knowing she likes licorice too, I offered her one.

"I still think you're a waste of space," she said, chewing.

Now I heard Heather go into her room. She was probably texting Jennifer or watching old episodes of *The Office*. I worked up my measly courage and walked over to her door.

Imagine this as a horror story. *He could hear his own teeth chattering with fear.*

I knocked.

"Who is it?"

"Ferris Bueller. I'm on my day off."

"Get lost."

"I just have something to ask you. It'll take like two and a half minutes tops."

"Fine. Come in but do not—I repeat, do not—touch anything. Don't even *look* at anything."

I slowly opened the door. She was sprawled on her bed with one earbud in and her laptop open. Heather's room hadn't changed much from the last time I was inside it. There was a row of glass animals on a shelf and some band posters taped to the wall. The only new thing was that she had taped up the magazine cover I had left her.

"I *said* don't look at anything."

My eyes went down to my feet.

"And hurry up. You're smelling up my room."

"Okay. Do you know anyone in high school with the initials G. O.?"

"Is this a serious question?"

"Yes."

"Let me think. Gary Ogilvy. Now get out."

"No, it's a girl."

"Please don't tell me you have a crush on an older girl. Because that would be the most singularly disgusting thing I've ever heard in my life."

"I don't have a crush."

"I just remembered a girl with those initials. Gloria Oxenberg. Now you can get out."

"Really? What's she like?"

"She's captain of the girls' basketball team."

"Does she like art or poetry?"

"Well, in English class she thought that *The Catcher in the Rye* was a book about farming."

I myself had no idea what *The Catcher in the Rye* was about. "Does she have blue hair? And is she Chinese or something?"

"Why, are you a racist?"

"No!"

"Gloria Oxenberg is tall, has a blonde ponytail, and is probably a lesbian in case that's also a problem for you. And if you ever try to speak to her, I have no doubt she'll pummel you into the ground for having a revolting personality."

"Is there any other girl with those initials?"

"Look, wingnut. High school isn't your baby middle school. It's big. It's like an Amazon warehouse for teenagers. You can get lost in the building. There are a thousand kids. I don't even know the names of everyone in my own classes."

"Oh."

"Don't touch anything on your way out."

Heather put both earbuds in and touched the keyboard of her computer. The screen was turned away from me but I could see it in the mirror on the wall behind her. She was watching a video from our holiday at a rented cottage. The screen showed Heather floating on an air mattress by the dock of the lake. From under the water came a figure that began to splash her. It was Jackson. Heather began to splash him back, and then Jackson turned over the air mattress, sending her into the water.

"Why are you still here?" she asked without looking away from the screen.

15

Not Good Enough

Personally, I couldn't understand why Jackson would want to leave.

I mean, our parents were perfectly nice. On the annoying scale, they rated three out of ten. And Mom and Dad were both pretty good cooks. We each had our own room. Our allowance went up every year.

We had *two* streaming services.

So why did Jackson leave? Because he didn't like us? Because we weren't good enough?

My parents said that wasn't the reason. They said it especially wasn't about any of us kids. But I couldn't help wondering what Jackson thought of me. Sometimes we would have fun together, throwing a football in the backyard or watching one of those shows he liked, where people pulled pranks on their friends. He liked to collect vinyl records from the punk era and would play his new one for me and I would pretend to like it. Once when my parents were out and he was supposed to make dinner, he made all of us enormous ice cream sundaes with whipped cream.

But that was Jackson in a good mood. When he wasn't, he didn't yell or throw things. He just grew dark and silent. If I spoke to him, he wouldn't answer.

It was with Mom and Dad that he got angry. Not long before he ran away he had an argument with them at the dinner table. It had something to do with losing his new, expensive basketball sneakers. Jackson finally got up and knocked me half off my chair as he went by.

I suppose George was the least affected by Jackson being gone. There was such a big age difference between them that they lived in different universes. George looked up to Jackson the way somebody looks up to a movie star or sports hero, as brilliant but distant, like an actual star in the sky. After Jackson left, George still went on playdates and trips to the zoo. He had a noisy birthday party and went crazy with delight over his mound of presents.

As for my parents—well, their whole life changed. They stopped going out for dinner with friends. They dropped their ballroom dancing lessons, which I was now sorry I used to make fun of. They didn't talk as much, or smile as much—unless they saw one of us looking at them. They *tried* to be normal parents, but I knew that every moment was hard for them.

And then there was Heather. She never went to parties or movies anymore. She had dropped all of her friends but Jennifer and spent most of her free time holed up in her room. When some boy she used to talk about finally came to the door to ask her out, she told him that she was too busy. Then she went back to her room. She didn't become any nicer to me, though. If anything, she was even meaner.

As for me, I'd really only had one friend, and you already know who that was. I wanted to hate Zack, but somehow I couldn't. There was something about the look in his eyes when he avoided me that made me feel a little sorry for him. Like he wasn't so happy about it either.

One night my dad came into my room. He said this was a pretty tough time and that it was okay if we had more questions about Jackson than answers. It's really hard to understand another person, he said, especially a troubled person. For now it was enough for us to care about Jackson and hope he was all right, and to wish for him to come home. And to care about each other too.

I listened but I didn't know what to say back. I couldn't even say thanks or okay. But my silence didn't seem to bother Dad. He put his arm around me, and then he went out, saying, "Get some shut-eye, sailor."

He hadn't called me sailor in years.

16

The Quick Stop

Do you think I just waited for another card to come my way?

No, I did not.

Do you think that I looked for one wherever I went?

Yes, I did.

And do you think I found one?

Nope. Zip. Nada. Nothing. I scanned the sidewalks, I checked under flowerpots and garbage-can lids. I looked in trees, on ladders left outside, under cats lying on the ground. I had hoped that g.o. had actually let that last card blow past our house, wanting me to see it. That somehow she had found where I lived and would plant more cards for me to discover. No such luck.

All I could do was take out the four cards I already had and prop them up so that I could look at them. Maybe, I thought, there were no more cards. Maybe g.o. had become tired of making them. Maybe I ought to stop thinking about them and work on my final project instead.

In class, Ms. Gorham had slipped me a note just as the bell rang.

Hartley,

Our final project presentations are starting on Monday. Please come see me after school tomorrow. That's the deadline for telling me your subject. I'm in real suspense!

Ms. Gorham

She was in suspense. Imagine how I felt. I read the note at my locker and then went to pick up George. On our walk home he talked exclusively about spiders. Or rather, he asked questions about them. Why did spiders have eight legs rather than seven, fourteen, or a hundred and forty? Did they go to spider school to learn how to make webs? Did flies taste good or did spiders want to throw up every time they had a meal?

I won't give you my answers, but believe me when I say I'm no entomologist.

George often asked me to play with him at home, but most of the time I had better things to do. But today I actually offered, remembering what my dad said about us caring about each other. I knew that my good intentions hadn't lasted very long, but I could still act on them now. Of course George was thrilled, so we sat on the floor in his room making robots out of LEGO. We worked with concentration, and as soon as they were done, we had them fight one another until they fell apart.

Mom and Dad came home at the same time and we ran down to see them.

"We played robots and now I'm *starving*," George said.

"Me too," I added.

"Well, no wonder," Dad said. "Anybody got an idea for dinner?"

Heather came down the stairs. "How about we go to Pizza Pantastic?"

George and I began to chant. *"Pizza Pantastic, Pizza Pantastic!"*

"A rare moment of agreement in the Staples household," Mom said. "Even if I do hate the name. Let's go!"

We went out to the car. George climbed onto his booster seat between me and Heather, and Dad pulled out of the driveway. We passed front lawns. Flowers blooming. An old lady on her porch knitting.

A card.

At least, I thought it was a card. It sure looked like one, stuck between the spokes of a tricycle that was tipped over on the sidewalk.

I shouted.

"STOP!"

Dad slammed on the brakes. The car screeched to a halt and we felt ourselves thrown against the seatbelts.

"What is it?" Dad cried. "A dog? A child? I didn't see anything!"

"Wait," I said. I opened the door and bolted out, ran down the sidewalk, and pulled the card—yes, it *was* a card—from between the spokes. I put it in my shirt pocket and sprinted back.

Mom turned in her seat. "Listen to me, mister," she said in her sternest voice. "Never, and I mean *never* run out of the car like that."

"For heaven's sake, you almost gave me a heart attack," Dad said. "What was it even about?"

"I thought I saw a five-dollar bill lying on the sidewalk. But it was just a leaf."

"You need to have your eyes checked," Heather said.

"I could have had an accident," Dad said. "Mom's right. Don't ever do that again, Hartley."

"Sorry."

Dad drove on.

"That was *so* fun," George said.

I had to wait until we had ordered our pizza and then eaten it, and George had finished his bowl of Neapolitan ice cream, for us to go home again.

I got another lecture about dangerous car behavior.

We pulled into the driveway. Heather went to her room to call Jennifer. Mom said George was so sticky with ice cream that if he didn't have a bath he'd become a mummy in his bedsheets. Dad went to check his email, which meant that he was going to see if anyone had sent him information about Jackson.

I said that I had to work on my final project. When my mom asked what it was about, I put my finger to my lips. "Top secret," I whispered.

In my room, I turned on the desk lamp and put down the card.

I liked the way the two people were moving through the air. I read the words. Sometimes I felt that way—about me and everyone else in the world going in different directions. But maybe everybody felt that way sometimes. Maybe Jackson really felt that way.

when i am going down, you are going up.

when i am going up, you are going down.

why can't we ever go in the same direction?

g.o.

6

g.o. was pretty insightful, if not exactly a laugh riot.

As usual, I took out the metal box and laid all the cards down so I could see them together. I wondered how many copies she made of each card. Did other people find them too? What did they do with them?

Maybe they used them as bookmarks.

Or as coasters to put their drinks on.

Maybe I had the only collection of g.o. in the world.

17

Have you ever woken up with a feeling of doom? I mean, you're not even awake enough to know what day it is but you just sense that it's a mistake to open your eyes. And that if you do open your eyes, you're going to see one of those big, sharp scimitars from *Aladdin* swinging just above your head?

I made myself open my eyes anyway. And then I remembered. Today I had to tell Ms. Gorham the subject for my final project.

As I dressed, I tried to come up with a subject.

Why are rooms rectangles instead of triangles or hexagons?

Why is a bedroom named after the bed when the kitchen isn't called the stoveroom?

These were not questions I was passionate about.

Walking to school with George, I told him my problem. "And today is the deadline," I said despondently. "I have to tell Ms. Gorham."

"How about doing it on your bum?" said George. "Bums are really interesting. Ha ha ha!"

He gave his fake laugh. Served me right for telling him. I took him to the elementary school entrance and then went around to the middle school side.

"Hey, Hartley!"

I looked and saw Stephanie Losurdo. She was holding the end of a skipping rope while her friend Louise Chong held the other.

"Want to try skipping?"

"I don't think I'd be very good at it," I said.

"You never know until you try. You might be a natural!"

Did Stephanie really think I might be a natural? Skipping had always looked fun to me. Besides, I could use something to take my mind off the final project. "Okay, I guess."

"Great. We'll start turning the rope and you just jump in."

The girls began to turn the rope, slowly at first and then faster. I put down my backpack and set my feet as if I were about to start a race. I held my breath, ran forward, and jumped in.

Smack! The rope hit me in the forehead. It slid down to my feet.

"Subject number twenty-four," said Stephanie. "Failure."

"What are you doing?" I asked.

"Oh, it's just a little experiment for my final project. You know how *passionate* I am about skipping, don't you, Hartley?"

"Terrific," I muttered, picking up my backpack and heading into school.

It's common sense that if you have a problem, you should try and figure out a solution. But maybe the opposite is sometimes true. If you think too much, you only get in a worse muddle. I thought all day about subjects for my final project. The history of chalk? How shoelaces are made? Why people say hello? It felt as if all the wires in my brain were tied in knots.

The final bell rang. I had no choice but to trudge over to Ms. Gorham's classroom. She was standing on a stepladder, putting up a big, colorful banner.

*** Final Project Extravaganza!***

Sometimes Ms. Gorham went a little overboard.

"Hartley, come in."

I shuffled up to her desk. She smiled in an encouraging way.

"Next week is the last week of school. And also when we get to see the final presentations. You won't have a lot of time to prepare, but I'll schedule you at the end. I'm so looking forward to hearing what subject you've chosen."

"Me too."

"That's funny, Hartley. So what is it? What's your subject?"

"Ah . . ."

Something caught my eye. A movement outside the classroom window.

Blue hair. Rolling by. Like the person was on a skateboard. It was her! It was g.o.!

"I'm sorry, Ms. Gorham, I've got to go!"

"What?"

"It's an emergency!"

I sprinted to the door.

"But what's your subject?"

I blurted out the first thing that came into my head.

"Tractors! My subject is tractors!"

If Ms. Gorham said anything in reply, I didn't stick around long enough to hear it. I raced down the hall, hoping a teacher wouldn't see me, and slid across the polished floor to the front doors. Yanking one open, I almost tumbled down the steps.

To the sidewalk.

Down to the corner.

Nothing.

She was gone. I didn't even know which direction. Even if I did, I couldn't keep up with her skateboard. Feeling defeated, I went around the school to pick up George at the other entrance.

George waved at me like a maniac. I thanked his teacher for standing with him and we began to walk home.

"Today I built a really, really tall tower," he said.

"That's nice."

"Then I knocked it down. *Kablooie!*"

"Ah-huh."

"Then I built it again."

"Right."

"Then I knocked it down. *Smash!*"

"Okay."

"Then I built it again."

"I get it, George."

"Also, I did a finger painting with my nose."

"I wondered what that orange spot was."

"And I found a fan. It keeps me really cool."

He began fanning himself.

"It's a million, trillion times better than air commissioning."

"I think you mean air conditioning."

"I just love my fan. See?"

He started to fan me, his hand too close to my face.

"Can you stop that?"

"Fine. I'll just fan myself."

He moved his hand with genteel little motions. Whatever he was waving, it wasn't a real fan.

It was a card!

"Where did you get that?"

"Found it."

"Where?"

"Dunno."

"Can I have it?"

"But it's my wonderful, beautiful fan."

"Please stop waving. It might get bent. I'll trade you for it."

George stopped. He put the card behind his back. "Trade me what?"

"I have a Choochoo bar at home."

"Thanks, but no thanks."

"How about my yo-yo? The one that lights up."

"The light doesn't even work anymore."

"A cowboy hat?"

"Blah."

"Well, what do you want?"

With his free hand George rubbed his chin. He was thinking so hard I half expected smoke to come out of his ears.

"*L'il Donkey.*"

"My comics? Okay, you can have one."

"Not just one."

"I'll give you two. Three."

"I want *all* of them."

"Oh, come on!"

"This really is such a nice fan," George said, waving it wildly around.

"All right, all right! You can have them all. Now hand over the card."

"Not until I have the comics."

"Walk faster, then."

But he didn't hurry up. He began to walk like an alien, with weird arm and leg movements, gurgling and beeping with each step. At last we reached home. We went upstairs and I opened my drawer and handed over all my *L'il Donkey* comics. It broke my heart to see them go.

some people
want to
believe

magic is real.

i
just
want
to
believe

that
i
am

g.o.

7

George immediately sat on my floor with them on his lap and opened the one on top.

"What do you think you're doing? Give me the card—I mean, the fan—and go to your own room."

So much for being nicer. George got up, stuck out his tongue, and handed me the card. As soon as he was out I closed the door. I went to my desk, turned on the lamp, and put the card down.

I pondered it for a long time.

"I believe in you, g.o.," I whispered.

18

g.o.

Her mother lived on the other side of town. Ever since her parents had split up she had lived in two places, with her dad during the week because he worked at home and with her mom, who was a law clerk in an office, on the weekends. She had to be careful to make sure she spent enough time with both of them so that nobody's feelings got hurt. Sometimes it felt to her as if she was the adult in the family.

She had come to her mom's house after school on Friday and now it was Saturday morning. She helped tidy up from breakfast and then told her mother that she needed to go to the mall to replenish her art supplies. Her mom offered to drive her, but she said no thanks and that she'd be back in time for them to have lunch together. Then she got her skateboard from the closet and glided down the drive while her mom watched from the window.

This card-making business had turned out to be pretty interesting. Just yesterday after school she had made a new card, one copy of which remained in the pocket of her hoodie. She needed some more construction paper in different colors and a new glue stick for whenever inspiration struck again.

It was too far to skate all the way, so she went three blocks to the bus stop and waited for a bus to arrive. She rode to the discount mall, where there was a big dollar store with an art supply aisle. The bus door opened with a hydraulic whoosh and she stepped down to the sidewalk. She stuffed her skateboard into her backpack and started to cross the mall parking lot. There was a seagull standing alone in the lot and she smiled, for it reminded her of the card in her pocket. It looked at her and opened its beak to make that lonely call that reminded her of the ocean. But there was no ocean around for hundreds of miles so what was it doing here?

And that was when she saw them.

They had been standing behind a minivan, one of the few cars in the lot. Either they'd been hiding or else doing something they didn't want anyone to see, but now they just stood watching her. Three of them.

They were all girls her age and they had been tormenting her ever since middle school. First it had been making fun of her heritage, calling her names. Then it had been making fun of her being adopted, saying that she'd been unwanted or worse. After becoming bored with just insults, they started to become physical. They bumped her in the school hall or tripped her or knocked the books from her arms. She had to always be looking ahead through the crowd, or over her shoulder, and she would hurry out of school as soon as the bell rang. The skateboard became her quick getaway. Maybe she could have told somebody—they certainly talked about bullying often enough in her school. But her parents had gone through their divorce and after that her dad had suffered his accident, followed by months of recovery and rehabilitation. The last thing she wanted was to add to her parents' problems.

So there they were: Noreen, Layla, and Starr. And as she walked toward the mall entrance they moved into her path, even while pretending not to look at her.

In the books and movies about bullying, it always turned out that the bullies had problems of their own. That they were acting out because of some personal unhappiness. Maybe that was true, but right now she could have cared less what Noreen's, Layla's, and

Starr's problems were. She didn't see any reason why they had to pick on her.

She veered left to walk toward another entrance. The three moved over to match her. Maybe she should turn around and run. Or drop her skateboard. She'd certainly gotten away from them before. She didn't believe that running made her a coward. She believed in self-preservation.

But she really needed those art supplies. So she kept going.

"Look who's here," said Noreen, making a move toward her.

"It's that girl from our school," Layla said. "Hey, how come you don't use chopsticks at lunch?"

Starr giggled. Starr was strictly a follower and didn't say much, glad to do anything that the others did. Noreen was definitely the leader. And the biggest too.

"What are you going shopping for?" Noreen asked, putting out a hand like a claw to catch her shoulder and pressing down hard.

"Probably some makeup to cover that ugly face," said Layla.

"Really ugly," Starr agreed.

Noreen dug in harder, and she winced from the pain. Maybe this was the time they would finally beat her up. And after that it would be easy to hurt her whenever they could.

No.

She gritted her teeth.

The fingers of her right hand made a fist.

She smacked Noreen in the right shoulder.

"Ow!"

It hadn't been that hard a punch, but Noreen let go. So she took off, running between the other two, straight to the entrance as fast as she could go. She reached the glass doors, pulled one open, and practically threw herself inside. There was no way they would follow her in here.

But when she turned around, there they were, fighting one another to get through the door. Noreen, first, ran toward her.

She turned and sprinted away, down the fake street that ran down the mall, her hoodie flapping. The few shoppers inside stopped to stare at her. Behind her she could hear the clomping sound of three pairs of shoes and their breathless urging one another on.

She kept going, running past the stores toward the food court, and as she maneuvered between the tables, her hoodie got caught on the back of a chair. When she yanked it, the card in the pocket flew out and landed on the table.

She wanted to take a step back to get it, but now she heard Noreen shout, "Get her!" So she jumped forward and powered toward the exit at the end of the food court. She shoved the door open with her shoulder, even as she wrestled her skateboard from her backpack. The board hit the ground and a second later she was rolling into the parking lot. From around the corner came a blue Subaru so she did a quick kick-turn and went the other way, crossing the lot and hopping onto the sidewalk.

And then she got a lucky break because the return bus was just pulling up to the stop. She picked up her skateboard, climbed the stairs, and deposited her ticket. And as the bus drove on, she looked through the window at the three girls standing in the parking lot, catching their breath and watching her pull away.

She thought of holding up her hand and making a rude gesture, but her parents had brought her up to know better.

19

Tractors?

Did I have to say *tractors*?

I couldn't have said fireworks or chimpanzees or Arctic exploration? What in the world made me say tractors? I couldn't imagine a subject that I felt *less* passionate about. I didn't know a single thing about them.

I was thinking this while staring at the waffle on my plate. It was Saturday morning, and the tradition was for Dad to get out the deluxe Belgian Waffle maker, mix a bowl of batter, and fill the kitchen with the sweet smell and sizzle. During the first couple of months after Jackson ran away, the tradition was forgotten, but then Dad started it up again.

As I looked down at the perfectly made waffle, softer in the middle and crisper at the edges, about to reach for the maple syrup, a hand came down and grabbed the waffle right off my plate.

"Hey! You thief!"

Heather looked down at me as she took a big bite of the waffle. She was wearing the red-and-white striped uniform of Pow Pow Popcorn.

"Mmm," she said, her mouth full.

"Don't worry, there's more where that came from," Dad said, pouring more batter onto the grill.

Heather leaned over again, picked up my milk, and swigged half of it down.

"Don't want to be late for work," she said. "Oh, by the way, Hartley, I keep meaning to tell you. There *is* another person in high school with those initials. And it's a girl."

"Seriously? Who is she? What's her name?"

"Sorry, got to go!"

She put the rest of the waffle in her mouth and ran out the door.

"Look at me!" said George. "I'm just like Heather."

He began stuffing his waffle into his mouth. I pushed back my chair and sprang up to follow. But by the time I got outside Heather was already on her bike. She waved at me as she glided down the driveway.

I went back inside. "Here's your waffle replacement," Dad said.

But I had lost my appetite. Heather would never tell

me. I just sat there dejectedly, but when I looked up again, I saw Mom staring at me.

"Don't tell me," she said. "You have a crush on another girl."

"Mom!"

"Just asking."

I hate the word *crush*. But in case you're wondering, fine, I did like a girl last year. Her name was Emma Suskind and she had long brown hair, a slight lisp, and played the flute. On the very last day of school, I finally got my courage up to ask if she wanted to go to a movie or for ice cream or something. But as I came up, I heard her tell a friend that she was moving with her family to Iceland.

So now you know.

Even though I wasn't hungry, I doused the waffle in maple syrup and began to chew a piece. An idea came to me.

"You know what would be a nice family outing this morning?"

"What?" said Dad.

"The mall. The one where Heather works. We can say hi to her."

"Funny, Hartley," said Mom. "You of all people wanting to go to the mall. The boy who hates to shop."

"No, I mean it. I need new undershirts."

"You don't even wear undershirts," Dad said.

"That's because I don't have any."

"I could get that baby present for my cousin," Mom said.

"I want to ride Dumpy!" cried George.

George meant the mechanical baby elephant in front of the hardware store. It wasn't really called Dumpy. That was just George's name for it.

"Why not?" said Dad, taking off his apron. "Let's all go to the mall."

Heather didn't work in the big mall that had the famous chain stores in it. She worked at the Whirton Discount Mall just off the old highway. It had stores like Factory Reject Fashion, Books by the Pound, and Ethel's Affordable Pets. When I was little, Jackson convinced me that at Ethel's you could buy a lizard with one eye, a guinea pig that barked, or a goldfish that swam upside down.

We drove to the mall and because it was early, and because most people went to the other mall, we got a parking space right by the door. Mom headed to the Good Deal Gift Gallery for her baby present while George dragged Dad off to ride Dumpy. I told them I wanted to wander a bit on my own.

I went straight to the food court at the far end. There

was 3-4-1 Sushi, Cheapo Burger, and Pow Pow Popcorn. Heather was behind the counter, wearing a paper hat and scooping popcorn into paper bags. I knew that she hated when we came to see her at work, so I was a little nervous to go up to the counter. I could even feel my stomach start to hurt. But I made myself go.

"Hi, sis," I said.

"What are you doing here? Scram."

A woman came up behind me. She had a shopping bag in each hand. "Are you going to order?" she asked me.

"Yes. Yes, I am," I said. "Excuse me, Miss, can you tell me what flavors you have?"

Heather glared at me. "We have cheezy-wheezy, candy crunch-crunch, pickle-wickle, and voom-voom vinegar."

"And what sizes do you have?"

"We have big, extra-big, jumbo, extra-jumbo, and giant."

"Do you have a small?"

"No, our smallest is a big."

"Your smallest is a big?"

"That's what I said."

"How big is big?"

"Not that big. More like a medium."

"Your big is a medium?"

"I really don't have time for this," huffed the woman behind me. She turned and marched over to Cheapo Burger.

"See that?" Heather growled. "You just made me lose a customer."

"I'll go away as soon as you tell me who the other person with the initials G. O. is."

"So you can stalk her?"

"That isn't funny. Can't you just tell me? Please?"

"All right, if it means you'll get out of here. Her name is Gretchen Oyster. She's fifteen and in the year below me. But Jennifer knows her from the student magazine. She's one of those artsy types, always hanging around the art room, member of the writing club. I think she was adopted from China when she was a baby. That is every last thing I know about her."

"Okay. Thanks, Heather."

"Actually, one more thing. She lives at 146 Almond Avenue. Do you want a bag of popcorn? It's on the house."

"Sure! I'll have voom-voom vinegar. Wait, that might be too sour. I'll have candy crunch-crunch. Unless it's the kind that gets stuck in your teeth—"

"Forget it," Heather said, turning back to the popcorn maker.

I didn't care about not getting any Pow Pow popcorn. Because now I knew who g.o. was.

Gretchen Oyster.

I walked away from the counter and sat at one of the food-court tables. The table was bolted to the floor. The chairs were bolted to the floor too. Just in case I wanted to steal one, I guess.

But I tried not to think about Gretchen Oyster. I tried to think about my final project and how I was going to get it done. I didn't have any information on tractors. Ms. Gorham didn't like us to use only the Internet, which meant that I was going to have to find information somewhere else. I could only hope that the less-than-impressive Whirton Public Library had something.

Only I wasn't at the library. I was at the mall.

My parents had said they would meet me here, but so far there was no sign of them. I knew that Heather would hate it if I watched her making popcorn, so I made sure to look in another direction. I gazed at one storefront after another and then at the tables around me, each one bolted to the floor. At home, George was always bumping into the kitchen table or just pushing it for no reason. Maybe we ought to bolt ours down too.

I noticed something on the table to the left of me.

Wouldn't it be cool if I found a card at the discount mall? How likely was that? Probably the odds were a million to one. Or worse.

It was the right size and shape of a card. But it was blank. Unless of course it was upside down.

Probably it was one of those little signs that stores stick onto a display: Rock Bottom Price! or Last One!

It wouldn't hurt to look, I supposed. I got up and took a step toward it.

It still looked like a possible card.

I shot over and picked it up, turning it over quickly. Yes! I couldn't believe my luck. I had the name of Gretchen Oyster *and* I had another card.

Reading the card, I realized something.

I realized that Gretchen Oyster was sad. She wasn't sad in the way I felt some of the time, or the way my parents felt most of the time, even if they tried to hide it. She was sad in her own way.

And I had another thought. I didn't need to feel the exact same thing as Gretchen Oyster to like her cards.

"Hey there, Hartley."

I looked up and saw Mom, Dad, and George coming

i would like to be

a bird

looking down

then everything

would be

so

clear

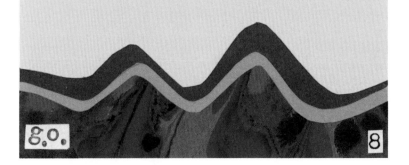

g.o.

8

toward me. I put my hand over the card and slid it off the table.

"We're going to say hi to Heather," Mom said. "Maybe she'll give us some free popcorn."

"Don't count on it," I replied.

20

Cat Paintings

We drove home and I discovered the not very surprising fact that my parents didn't know anything about tractors. George, however, did offer this nugget:

"They're strong like me!"

Then he lowered his head, made the sound of an engine, and began shoving his hands against me.

I asked Dad to drop me off at the Whirton Public Library on the way home. The mobile home looked the same as always, except that now there was a sign handwritten in the window that said We Do Not Need Any More Fishing Magazines.

As soon as I walked in a voice called out, "Is that you, Ricky Stackhouse?"

"No, Mrs. Scheer. It's me again, Hartley Staples."

Mrs. Scheer peered through the doorway of her office at me. "Are you sure you're not Ricky Stackhouse?"

"Absolutely, Mrs. Scheer."

"All right, then. But if you see Ricky Stackhouse give me a holler. Or if you see Mr. Scheer."

"Your husband?"

"If you see Mr. Scheer come up the steps, you just bar the way. Do you hear me? You bar the way!"

"What did Mr. Scheer do?"

"Only bend over the corner of a page, that's all."

"To mark his place?"

"That's right. Too lazy to get a bookmark or a leaf or a piece of toilet paper. Bent the corner right over. One of our best books on ghosts. Now he's banned for a month. We play no favorites here."

Being a librarian was starting to sound like being a police officer. I started to look on the shelves. There was no section on agriculture or machines, but there was a shelf called Things That Make Loud Noises and, sure enough, there was the book I was looking for.

Your Friend, the Tractor.

I took it off the shelf and saw that the cover was held on by clear tape curling at the edges. It smelled like an old pair of rubber boots, which isn't actually too bad. It had been published in 1962 and the first photograph was of a farmer with a brush cut and wearing overalls as he stood beside his tractor.

When I got home, I put the new card into the metal box. I planned to read the entire tractor book by the end of the weekend, but on Sunday Mom and Dad insisted that we all go to the town square to see the Whirton Outdoor Art Show. Local artists had their art on display and stood there hoping that somebody would buy something. To prevent death by boredom, I made a survey of the most popular subjects painted by Whirton artists.

1. Cat sleeping on a chair
2. Cat awake on a chair
3. Clown holding a flower
4. Clown eating a flower
5. Cat wearing a clown's hat

Then we had to go for a picnic, and then a walk, and when we finally got home, Mom asked me to cut the grass. That left only about half an hour before dinner. I went up to my room and sat at my desk.

The book, *Your Friend, the Tractor*, lay before me.

I pushed it aside and took out the metal box. Then I laid out the cards that I had, all seven of them. I read the words on each one.

If only I had number 3. It was like missing a piece of a puzzle you just spent three hours making, only worse.

"Dinner!" called Dad. The cards went back into the metal box. I hadn't spent even five minutes on my final project.

21

The Curveball

On Monday morning the presentations began. I expected Ms. Gorham to arrive in a top hat and spangles, like the ringleader of a circus. I imagined her saying, *"And now ladies and gentlemen, for your entertainment . . ."*

Okay, so she didn't arrive in a top hat. And she didn't say those words. But she might as well have, the way she whipped everyone up with excitement. "This is it," she said, standing in front of her desk. "It's the day we've all been waiting for. Your final projects. The last work you need to do before graduating middle school. Is this a big deal?"

"Yes it is!" everyone shouted.

"Are we excited?"

"Yes we are!"

"All right, then. Let's get started."

Max Purcell went first. He had to because he was getting overheated in his homemade space suit. It sort of looked like the one worn by Neil Armstrong to walk on the moon—that is, if Neil Armstrong had worn a white painter's outfit and had an old suitcase strapped to his back and a hockey helmet on his head. The helmet had gold wrapping paper taped on the inside of the visor. Unable to see, Max kept crashing into things.

After him came Simon Asch on the history of baseball. He showed us a black-and-white film of Babe Ruth. He told us about Hank Greenberg and Jackie Robinson. He demonstrated a curveball, throwing it across the room to Marianne Warner who had brought her catcher's mitt. But Simon threw wide and the ball smacked the back wall and bounced into Delmore Hass's nose.

Delmore went to see the nurse.

Lauren Engerer displayed an enormous banner that showed every dog breed in the world. Who knew that a Japanese Chin was cousin to a King Charles Spaniel? She added some excellent barking and yipping imitations that were sure to get her bonus marks.

The next day, the presentations continued. Terrance Borne gave a talk on the history of 1960s folk music and played a song that he made up called "How Fragile the Peach." It was about the planet Earth being like a peach and how we had to be careful not to bruise it. Ms. Gorham called it "deep."

Celia Horngold informed us that pencil erasers could be made out of real or synthetic rubber. Ms. Gorham asked her which was better. "I don't know," Celia said and started to cry.

On Wednesday Zack Mirani—well, I don't know what Zack Mirani did his presentation on because I put my fingers in my ears.

Samuel Swenton told us about the horror of poison gas in World War I. Then he lit a stink bomb before Ms. Gorham could stop him.

As always, I picked up George after school. When we got home, I was surprised to see Heather lying on the front lawn and looking up at the sky.

"Hmm," said George, looking down at her. "Should I lie down outside or watch television? Outside or television? I know. Television!"

He ran inside. But I stayed out. I watched Heather for a while, and since she didn't tell me to buzz off, I got down on the grass beside her and lay down too. I could feel the blades tickling my neck. In the sky I saw an enormous, football-shaped balloon.

"Is that a UFO?" I asked.

"It's a dirigible," Heather said.

"A what?"

I expected her to call me stupid but she didn't. "An airship. It's filled with helium. There's a cabin underneath for the pilot and passengers. There are these giant fans that move it in one direction or another."

"How do you know that?"

"Jackson told me once."

"He knows a lot about airplanes and stuff like that."

Heather sighed. "He's not coming back, you realize."

"You don't know that."

"Everybody is just waiting for him to come home. But he's not going to. Why would he? If he liked living with us, he wouldn't have left in the first place. He probably never even thinks about us."

"That isn't true."

"Because we're twins, everybody always thought I knew what he was thinking. But I didn't. I never knew. He was always different from me. It didn't mean we weren't connected. I mean, he was always there with me, even before I can remember. Me as a baby, Jackson as a baby. Hearing him breathe in the crib beside me. Always there. That's the thing that hurts, that there's this space where he used to be, where the thing that I was always sure of used to be. Now it's empty. And I want to get over it. I need to. I can't stand living like this."

She stood up. "What are you doing?" I asked.

"I need to move."

She got on her bike, which was leaning against the porch steps, and rode away down the sidewalk. I sat up to watch her disappear. What if she didn't come back? What if my parents didn't come home from work? What if all the things I thought were certain turned out not to be?

But I didn't do anything, just lay back down and stayed there for a long time. I stayed there staring up at the clouds, which didn't look like a dog or a shoe or anything else the way they had when I was little, but just like clouds.

22

Now or Never

I woke up.

I opened my eyes.

I screamed.

That is, I screamed inwardly. But it was the loudest silent scream I ever made. Because today was the last day of school and the last day to present our final projects. Which meant that it was the day *I* had to present.

I thought of dressing like someone who would use a tractor, but I didn't have overalls or a straw hat, and anyway, I didn't know if that was really how tractor drivers dressed anymore. Everything I knew stopped at 1962, the year that *Your Friend, the Tractor* was published, and I hadn't even finished reading it. I put on my regular clothes and went downstairs, vowing not to tell anyone in my family that I had to present today.

I sat down at the table between George and Heather and poured myself a bowl of cereal. "My throat is feeling kind of scratchy," I said. "I might be getting sick. I might have strep throat. Or maybe pneumonia."

"I know what you have," Heather said. "You have a case of faker-itis."

"What?"

"You're so funny, Hartley," Mom said. "We know that today's the big day."

"Big day?"

"Don't be coy with us, young man," Dad said in a joking tone.

My father looked over at my mother and together they said—*"It's final project day!"*

I jerked up in my seat. "How do *you* know that?"

"We got an email from your teacher," Mom said. "She wanted to make sure that you were prepared. But I wrote back and said that you haven't asked us for help, and that means you're prepared. We know our boy."

"So what's your subject?" asked Dad. "You still haven't told us."

I looked down into my increasingly soggy cereal. "Tractors."

"Ha, ha. You made that joke before. No, really. What's it on?"

"I mean it. My project is on tractors."

Dad looked at me.

Mom looked at me.

"Good luck with that," Heather said, getting up and grabbing her backpack. She patted me on my head. "I mean it, Hartley. Because you're going to need it."

The whole way to school, George pretended to be driving a tractor. He made *vvvrrr, vvvrrr* noises and steered an imaginary wheel and shifted imaginary gears and, for some reason, deliberately ran into several trees. I sent him into school and then went around to my side. I didn't need to go to my locker because I already had the tractor book in my backpack. I walked down the crowded hall and bumped into someone.

"Sorry," I said.

The person turned to look at me. Zack Mirani.

"That's okay," he said, and immediately began an unconvincing coughing fit. For months I had let him avoid me, but this morning felt different. Maybe because it was the day of my final project. Maybe it was what Heather had said on the lawn yesterday. Maybe it was because I was just fed up.

I walked around him. "Hey, Zack."

"What?" (Cough, cough.)

"It's me, Hartley Staples. The guy you used to spend every lunch and every recess and every weekend with."

"Oh, right. Hi."

"So what's the deal?"

"The deal?"

"With not talking to me. Just because my brother ran away from home? Maybe you think it's contagious or something."

Zack is taller than me. He has really black hair, cut short, and his features are all sort of pointy. He tried not to look at me, but somewhere over my head.

"I don't think that."

"You do. You think that I'm a pathetic loser and not worth hanging out with anymore."

"I *don't* think that."

"I don't even know why I'm trying," I said. "I thought I already gave up. Never mind, Zack. Have a nice life."

"Wait," he said, and he put his hand on my arm. But he quickly let go again. "It's not me."

"I don't know what that means."

"It's not me. It's my parents. They told me that if I hung out with you anymore, or even talked to you, I couldn't go to Camp Birch Bark this summer."

I knew that Zack wanted to go to Camp Birch Bark until he was old enough to be a counselor.

"Is this for real?"

"It is. They gave me an ultimatum. They even called it that, an 'ultimatum.' You know where I have my lunch now? In the music room. Alone. Well, I guess I could talk to the cellos. I don't think there's anything wrong with you, Hartley. I miss hanging out too. At least you don't have to feel guilty about it the way I do."

"So now you want me to feel sorry for you?" I said. "Because you made the very, very difficult decision of choosing camp over me? Or because you couldn't tell your parents that they were just wrong and that you were going to stay my friend anyway? Because you wouldn't stand up to them?"

Zack still didn't look at me, but his pointy jaw started to tremble. And then a tear began to slip down his cheek. Cripes. First Ms. Gorham and now Zack. Was everybody I knew going to start crying when they talked to me?

Even though I didn't want to, I did start to feel kind of sorry for him. But it didn't make things right. "Whatever," I said. "At least I know the reason you pretend I'm invisible. Have a good time at camp."

"Hartley—"

I walked away. Only now did I see that the hall was deserted. The bell must have rung without my hearing it. I hurried to Ms. Gorham's class and slipped inside just as she was closing the door.

"Good morning, class. This is the final day of presentations. And you know what comes after that, don't you?"

Everyone shouted at once. *"PARTY!"*

Ms. Gorham gave us two thumbs-up. "That's right. We're going to have our final project celebration. You all deserve it for working so hard. We're going to have games and a movie and cake and ice cream."

"I'm gluten-free," said Lauren Engerer.

"I'm lactose intolerant," said Gavin Luo.

"I'm allergic to nuts," said Simon Asch.

"I don't eat meat," said Gerald Yacoubian.

"Don't worry, I've got you all covered," Ms. Gorham said. "Now who is our first presenter of the day?"

Stephanie Losurdo's hand shot up. She went to the front of the class and gave her presentation on the skipping rope. She told us that people skipped rope in early China and ancient Egypt. She and her friends demonstrated various skipping methods. The toe-to-toe. The scissors. The swing kick. Then she presented the results of her playground study.

"People who have never skipped before," she concluded, "are really bad at it."

After her came Jeffrey Markowitz on the invention of printing. He was dressed in costume as the first printer, Johannes Gutenberg, in a shirt with puffy sleeves and a velvet hat.

"Writing out a whole book by hand takes too long," Johannes Gutenberg declared. "There must be a better way. Wait a minute! Why don't I invent the printing press?"

People applauded. Ms. Gorham said, "And now for the very last presentation. Hartley Staples, please come up."

I grabbed my backpack and walked slowly to the front of the class. I turned around and looked at the class. Everyone looked back at me. Josephine Flax was scratching her nose. Even Zack looked at me.

"The tractor."

"Very good," Ms. Gorham said encouragingly.

"The tractor is a very interesting subject." I unzipped my backpack and reached inside.

I felt the metal box.

What was the metal box doing in my backpack? Where

was the library book? I felt around but the book wasn't there. Somehow I had put the box in instead.

Beads of sweat broke out on my forehead. What was I supposed to do now? Without the book, there was no way I could talk about tractors. The only thing to do was talk about g.o.'s cards. Of course, I had already decided not to talk about them, but this was an emergency. I could tell the class how I found them. I could display them on the shelf below the blackboard and let everyone get a close look. Then we could have a discussion about what they meant.

Only I couldn't. I didn't know why, but I couldn't.

"Ms. Gorham?"

"Yes, Hartley?"

"The truth is that I don't know very much about tractors. In fact, nothing."

A few kids laughed, but Ms. Gorham frowned. "Are you sure that you don't want to try?"

I just shook my head. Ms. Gorham rubbed her chin, clearly wondering what to do. I felt a lot of sympathy for her. It wasn't easy being a teacher. She knew my family was having a tough year and didn't really want to punish me. But everybody else had given a presentation.

I decided to make it easy for her.

"I guess you better send me to the office, Ms. Gorham."

"I'm not sure if that's necessary."

"I certainly shouldn't be allowed to enjoy the party."

"Well . . ."

"And cake. There's no way I should have cake."

"Perhaps just a small piece."

"Don't feel bad, Ms. Gorham. You're doing the right thing."

I picked up my backpack. I could feel the whole class staring at me as I went out and closed the door behind me.

23

Almond Avenue

I walked down the hall to the office and sat on the bench.

Behind the counter, a secretary was talking to a parent on the phone while another was handing a Band-Aid to a boy with a scraped elbow. Somebody came in to sign out for a doctor's appointment, while another student came back from her flute lesson.

I noticed that my backpack was still open so I bent over to close it. And what did I see but the book on tractors. It had been shoved behind the metal box. How had I missed it? I could have given my presentation after all. It would have been pretty lame, but at least I might have passed. Now I was probably going to fail eighth grade. I wouldn't be able to go to high school next year with the other kids my age.

I didn't have anything better to do, so I pulled out the book on tractors and started to read. I read for almost an hour before taking out my lunch. I kept reading even while I ate. One of the secretaries gave me a box of orange juice.

Another gave me a chocolate chip cookie. Tractors were actually pretty interesting. They had been built to replace horses for farmwork. The first tractors, built a hundred and fifty years ago, had used steam engines like the early trains.

At last the bell rang. A cheer went up in every classroom. School was over for the year. People began streaming into the halls. I wished that I could feel as happy as everyone else.

After thanking the secretaries, I went around to pick up George. He was holding a box of things that he had made in school.

"I have my music shakers," he said as we began to walk home. "I have my map of the world and my tin-foil sculpture and my potato-stamp pattern and my bead necklace . . ."

Imagine having to tell your parents that you needed to repeat eighth grade. Your parents who were already dealing with a missing kid. I could feel a stomachache coming on just thinking about it. Boy, were they going to be disappointed in me.

When we got to the house, Heather was just leaning her bike against the side of the porch. High school had already been over for a week. "So they finally let you out," she said.

"This has been a real red-letter day," I said.

"A what?"

"A red-letter day."

"What does that mean?"

To tell the truth, I wasn't sure. Today I got up in front of my whole class and made a fool out of myself. Today my former best friend told me that he had chosen Camp Birch Bark over me. It just seemed like the right expression, whatever it meant.

"Are you going to be home?" I asked.

"Where do you think I'm going—Paris, France?"

"Then you can stay with George. I have something to do."

"Like what?"

"It's been a red-letter day," I repeated, "and I have something to do. And I'm borrowing your bike."

"Excuse me?"

"Mine's too small."

"Oh, no, you're not."

But for once in my life, I was too fast for her. I grabbed the bike, pushed it off, and hopped onto the seat. It was a bit large for me, so that I had to stretch to reach the pedals. But I got up a good speed, and when I glanced back over my shoulder, I saw her and George standing on the driveway watching me go.

I stayed on the sidewalk, riding past the Whirton Middle School and the Whirton High School. It wasn't easy stopping for a stop sign. I had to brake and then reach out and grab the pole.

I knew where I wanted to go. Almond Avenue. I just wasn't a hundred percent sure that I knew how to get there. I thought it might be the street ahead, but when I got there and read the sign, I was wrong. So I kept going for two more blocks and then thought maybe I ought to give up, only I didn't want to give up, so I went two more.

And there it was. Almond Avenue.

I turned to the right but the numbers were too low and so I had to check for traffic before rolling onto the street to make a U-turn so that I could go the other way. I passed the intersection again and looked at the house numbers to make sure I was going in the right direction. The houses were smaller than the ones on our street, with tiny wooden porches and front gardens, but they were just as neat. I didn't have far to go to get to number 146, Gretchen Oyster's house.

When I got off the bike, it fell on top of me.

I almost expected the front of the house to be a collage, with people and fish floating across the front. But it was an ordinary house, painted a nice blue-gray and with a yellow door. As I stood looking at it, I remembered my sister asking if I was a stalker. Standing here and staring might seem to someone like weird behavior, so I walked up to the door. Walking up to the door was normal behavior.

The door didn't have a knocker, and there was no bell either, so I knocked. Probably too softly for anything but a mouse to hear.

I knocked again.

I knocked louder.

"Don't break it down," said a voice from the other side.

The door opened. It was her. The girl with the blue hair. Gretchen Oyster.

"Oh, hi," I said.

"We don't buy Boy Scout fudge, if that's what you're selling."

"I don't think the Boy Scouts sell fudge."

"Whatever."

"I'm looking for you, actually."

"Me?" She eyed me suspiciously. "Is this a trick? Did somebody send you? Because if Noreen and Layla and Starr sent you—"

"Nobody sent me."

"Well, you look kind of familiar."

"That's probably because I chased you the other day."

"Chased me?"

"You're Gretchen Oyster."

"How do you know my name?"

"My sister, Heather, told me. You don't actually know her; she's a year ahead of you in school."

"You're not making any sense."

"Let me try again. You're g.o. The initials. I have some of the cards you made."

Something changed in her. She got all stiff and alert. Quietly she said, "You do?"

"I have up to number 8."

"You have *all* of them?"

"Except for number 3. I never found that one. I really like them. I don't know if I understand them, exactly, but I think I appreciate them."

"Huh. Really. Thanks, I guess. Good-bye, then."

She started to close the door. I said, "Wait."

She opened the door again. "Do you want something?"

"I don't know," I said disconsolately. Suddenly, coming to meet Gretchen Oyster seemed like the most ridiculous thing I had ever done. What did I expect to happen? Maybe I was like some person who thought that if they could only meet their favorite movie star or musician, their life would be better. But of course it wasn't better. It wasn't even any different at all.

"You look kind of ill," she said.

"I have a stomachache."

"You better have a glass of water. Come in."

It seemed more like an order than a suggestion so I followed her. She took me to the kitchen and told me to sit down at the table. It was a small kitchen, with flower wallpaper on the walls and an old gas stove and glass jars with spices and things in them lined up at the back of the counter. She filled a glass at the tap and gave it to me.

I drank half the glass down, spilling a bit on my chin.

"You're the first person who has ever said anything to me about my cards."

"Maybe that's because nobody knows who you are."

"Good point."

"Do you make very many copies?"

"It depends on how much money I've made from mowing people's lawns. Usually I make ten or twenty."

"And you just leave them around for people to find?"

"Kind of lame, I know. Probably they just get thrown out or whatever. But I like the idea of somebody finding one and going, *hmm*. You know what I mean?"

"I think I do."

"So how old are you?" she asked. "What grade are you in?"

"Thirteen. I just finished eighth grade. Well, I didn't exactly finish because I didn't do my final project."

"Ms. Gorham's final project?"

"Uh-huh. Anyway, I'm going to show your cards to my older brother."

"Who?"

"You know, it's a funny thing, but I just figured that out right now. I'm collecting them so that I can show them to Jackson. If he comes back."

"You're very confusing, do you know that? Where's your brother?"

"He ran away."

"Your brother is *that* Jackson? Jackson Staples? Everybody in high school knows about him."

"Can I have some more water?" I asked.

She took the glass and filled it again. I managed not to spill this time. "I better get home. I'm sure you think I'm a freak or something, but you were nice anyway," I said.

I got up, and this time Gretchen Oyster followed me to the door. She said, "Which card don't you have?"

"Number 3."

"Hold on." She turned and ran up the stairs, taking two at a time. A minute or two later she came down again with a card in her hand. "I think I only made seven of these. This is the last copy."

"Thanks a lot. I'll look at it at home."

"What's your name?"

"Hartley Staples. But we don't own the store."

"Thanks, Hartley."

"For what?"

"For liking them."

"You're welcome. By the way, who are Noreen, Layla, and Starr?"

She made a face. "You don't want to know."

"Are they after you?"

"Something like that."

"Why?"

"I don't even know."

"Have you told somebody?"

"You," she said, opening the door. "I've told you."

I turned to her. "That's a start. Now you have to tell somebody else."

She looked at me as if *she* had a stomachache. I went outside but she didn't follow. This time I had a lot of trouble getting onto Heather's bike. But I finally managed and rode home carefully. I put the bike in the garage and then went into the house, past the family room where Heather and George were watching some cartoons, and up to my room.

As always, I put the card on my desk and turned on the lamp.

I thought it was a good one, and I was glad to have it.

you know

that sound

nobody else

hears?

it might

be near

or far

what is it?

all i know

is i hear it

too

go.

3

24

A Little Delay

Officially it was the start of summer. Only I didn't feel as if I had earned it—not yet, anyway. Biking home from Almond Avenue, even as I was thinking about Gretchen Oyster, I decided to delay my own summer.

Because I hadn't yet done my final project.

I knew that it was too late, that the teachers had already given in their students' final marks. In a couple of weeks report cards would be sent out to parents, and there would probably be my big, fat failing grade. I couldn't change that, but I could change how I felt, and so I decided to write a paper to take the place of my final project. If nothing else, I would gain back my self-respect.

For two days, I worked at the desk in my room. My parents kept coming up to my door. "It's summer, for goodness' sake. What are you doing in there?"

Besides the book, *Your Friend, the Tractor*, I had found some information in the encyclopedia we had in our house.

In Jackson's room there was a book on the development of the automobile that had a chapter on other kinds of vehicles. I used the Internet for more recent developments.

The paper ended up being fourteen pages, longer than any essay I had ever written before. Plus I added five pages of my own drawings, from the first steam engines to the giant, high-traction machines of today. The last thing I wrote was the conclusion. Maybe I got a little carried away.

The tractor might not be a glamorous vehicle,
like a Porsche or a jet airplane. But it gets the job
done. It helps the farmer to put food on our table, the
builder to prepare the land for a new house. It turns an
ordinary driver into someone with the strength of a
superhero. I say, let's give a cheer for the hardest
working machine around. Hip, hip hooray for
the tractor!

I finished it at one o'clock in the afternoon on Monday. My parents were both at work but Heather was home to watch George. I slipped the essay into a big envelope, went out the door, and walked to Whirton Middle School.

I knew that teachers didn't finish the school year on the same day as us. They had all kinds of paperwork to do and meetings to attend. I just had to hope that Ms. Gorham was still there.

As I got to the office, one of the secretaries was coming out the door with a cardboard box full of stuff. "Did you forget something, Hartley?" she asked.

"Kind of," I answered. "Is Ms. Gorham still here?"

"I think she's just packing up."

My footsteps echoed in the empty hallway. There were chairs piled here and there, mounds of paper garbage next to abandoned brooms. In one room a janitor on a ladder was taking down a burned-out fluorescent lightbulb.

I got to Ms. Gorham's room and looked in, but I didn't see anybody. Then I heard a rustling sound. Stepping inside, I saw her at the back, standing on her tiptoes in order to reach a poster. She was wearing blue jeans and a T-shirt, just like a regular person. She had a bandana tied around her hair.

"Ms. Gorham?"

She half-turned around. "Hartley? One second."

She finished pulling down the poster and then came toward me as she rolled it up. "There always seems to be one more thing to take down," she said. "But what are you doing here? You should be out in the sunshine."

I said, solemnly, "I'm sorry that I disappointed you."

"Oh, Hartley."

"I know it isn't your fault that you had to fail me and keep me in middle school. And I know it's too late to change my mark, but I wanted to do the final project anyway. So I wrote an essay for you."

I held out the envelope. She took it from me and pulled out the essay. "This looks interesting," she said. "Why don't you wait while I look it over? I can give you something to read."

"Okay," I said.

Ms. Gorham went to her desk and took a paperback from a box of stuff. She handed it to me. It was a slim book called *Animal Farm*.

I sat down at my old desk, which wasn't my desk anymore, and opened the book. It started like this: "Mr. Jones, of the Manor Farm, had locked the hen-houses for the night, but was too drunk to remember to shut the pop-holes." I couldn't remember ever reading a book that started with somebody being drunk. Also, I didn't know what pop-holes were.

But I kept reading. Mr. Jones went to bed and then there was a description of a big pig named Major. Some other animals too. It got interesting pretty fast, so that I didn't notice the time going by and only looked up when Ms. Gorham tapped me on the shoulder.

"This is a fine essay, Hartley."

"It is?"

"Informed, well-written, serious. And I loved the ending. I've circled a couple of grammatical errors, but that's all. I'm just so impressed that you did this on the first days of your holiday."

"Thanks for reading it," I said. Ms. Gorham took a pen out of her pocket, put the essay down on my desk, and wrote A+ on the first page. Then she handed it back to me.

"Of course you didn't fail, Hartley. You did good work all year. I wouldn't hold you back for missing one assignment. You're going to high school next year whether you want to or not."

"I am?"

Ms. Gorham gave me her best smile ever.

"Have a really great summer, Hartley."

25

So I was going to graduate middle school after all. I didn't have to repeat eighth grade. A flood of relief poured over me. I tucked the envelope with my first A+ (even if it didn't count) under my arm and started to walk home again.

But then, being me, Hartley Staples, I couldn't just be glad about it. Not even for one day. Because I had to start worrying about high school. In September I would have to enter that enormous building with a zillion other kids. I'd get lost every five minutes and have all new teachers, and some of them were bound to be a lot more strict than Ms. Gorham.

I was also going to have to make new friends, especially since I didn't have Zack Mirani to rely on anymore. Maybe one day Zack and I would be friends again. It didn't seem impossible, even if I couldn't see how we might get there. But I was starting to think that one friend wasn't enough and that a person needed more.

Backups, you might say, just in case one of them pulled a Zack Mirani on you.

I shook myself, trying to get all these thoughts out of my head. After all, it really was the summer now. I didn't have to think about school for two months. I could actually enjoy myself. Not that my family was really big on enjoyment these days, but I know my parents were trying. I guess that I'd have to find a way to help them.

Our house came into view. Even though it was still early afternoon, the car was in the driveway. That was strange—my parents should have both been at work. They weren't taking any holiday time yet.

I got to the door and when I opened it I could hear voices in the living room. Somebody was talking. Mom and Dad were sitting on the sofa, facing a visitor who sat in the armchair. The visitor had long hair, but even before he turned around, I knew that it was Jackson.

George was sitting on the rug beside him. I just stood there, not knowing what to do. My parents looked up at me but it was a moment before Mom said anything.

"Hartley. There you are."

Jackson turned around. He looked different somehow, maybe just older. He gave me a big grin.

"Hey, Hartley! Look how tall you are. Come here, buddy."

But I couldn't move. I tried to say something but I couldn't even talk.

I started to cry. I guess now it was my turn.

Jackson came over and put his arms around me. "That's okay, Hartley," he said, "that's okay."

It took me another few minutes before I could speak. I said something really obvious. I said, "You're home."

"That's right."

"Are you going to stay?"

"I hope so. I want to."

Mom and Dad both smiled. "It's going to be okay, Hartley," Dad said.

"Where's Heather?" I asked.

"Oh, Heather," Jackson said in an embarrassed way. "She took one look at me and ran upstairs and locked herself in her room."

"Why?"

"Emotions are complicated, I guess."

I said, "I got an A+ on my final project." It was a stupid thing to mention, under the circumstances.

"In Ms. Gorham's class?" asked Jackson. "Way to go, Hartley. Quite the brainiac, you are."

"Maybe you should go upstairs and knock on Heather's door," I said. "She probably wants to see you."

"That's a good idea. Want to come with me?"

"I'll come!" said George.

"I think she probably wants to see you by yourself."

"You've gotten pretty mature, I see. Okay, I'll go up. Thanks for the advice."

"You're welcome. Hey, Jackson?"

"Uh-huh?" he said, getting up. I wanted to ask him about why he had left, and where he had been, and a million other things. But maybe it wasn't the right time.

"Never mind," I said.

He patted me on the head, like he used to do when I was little. Mom and Dad and George and I all watched as Jackson went up the stairs. We heard him knock softly on the door.

We heard the door open.

26

The next few days felt almost as strange as the days after Jackson ran away. I kept asking myself questions. Would he still be here at dinner? Was he actually going to sleep in his room? Would he be around the next afternoon, in the evening, in the morning?

And he was. I still didn't ask him where he had been all these months or what he'd been doing. Maybe my parents or Heather did, during the times they spent alone with him, but I'm not sure. When we were together, Jackson and I talked about ordinary things, like how the sports teams we liked were doing. I didn't really care that much about sports teams, but I kept up so that I could talk to Jackson and I had followed them even while he was away. Sports teams are pretty useful as a subject of conversation.

We also spent time as a family, especially in the kitchen. Jackson missed Mom's roast chicken, Dad's stir-fry, and just about every other dish we had at home. "This is the best hamburger I've ever had," Jackson would say. "This is the best tuna fish sandwich in the world." We made popcorn and watched dumb comedies on TV that made us laugh. We went to the store to pick up ice cream and ate big bowls of it in the backyard. When George got his bowl, he said, "I'm in ice cream heaven."

One night when I was reading *Animal Farm* in bed, my parents came in to talk. They said that all of us kids were being really great and also that it was natural for everything to feel weird for a while. My dad said that they weren't taking anything for granted, pretending that everything was all right now. Instead, they were going to make sure that they had help dealing with the problems that made Jackson want to leave. He had agreed to see a therapist, and also the family doctor for a full checkup to make sure he was in good health.

Mom said that there might be times when Jackson being home wasn't going to be as easy as it was right now. If that was true for me, then I should come and talk about it with them. She hoped I wouldn't mind if every so often they asked me how things were going, just to check in. And by the way, they were all going to go back to the family therapist for a little while, and if I wanted to talk to the therapist by myself that was all right too.

Both of them wanted me to know that Jackson had to get a lot of attention right now but that this family was about all of us. It was about me and George and Heather too. And if there was anything that I needed, anything that I was worried or unhappy about, I should let them know. It was okay to be worried or unhappy sometimes, of course, but still I could always talk to them.

"Don't worry," I said to them. "I'm not going to run away."

"I know," Mom said and hugged me.

Dad hugged me too.

Then they went out and I finished reading *Animal Farm*. It's a very good book.

27

Wishful Thinking

I'll be honest with you, the idea of giving Jackson the metal box of cards seemed to make more sense to me *before* he came home. I had this idea that he would love them and that they would be even more meaningful to him than they were to me, and that somehow they would help him to stay with us.

But now that he was back, all of that seemed like wishful thinking or plain dumb. Just because I liked them didn't mean he would. Or that they would mean something special. In my room, every time I picked up the box and thought of giving them to him, I felt myself getting all awkward and embarrassed. For all I knew, he would just laugh, as if he thought I was making some kind of joke.

And there was another thing. Maybe there was a part of me that didn't want to give them up.

But overall, I still wanted to give them to Jackson. It wasn't up to me to decide what he should think of them. *Just do it*, I told myself.

Only I couldn't just shove the box at him. Or do it only a few days after he got home. So I waited. I waited for over two weeks. It was Sunday and in the morning we went to Leaning Bear to hike. This time Jackson didn't run ahead like he used to, but stayed with everyone. At least he stayed until the last bit, when he couldn't stop himself from sprinting up to the top. He didn't try to go any farther than the rope, which I could see was a relief to my parents.

We came home again and had lunch. My parents went to take a nap, while George set up his Space Wars figures in the living room and Heather rode her bike to Jen's house.

I knocked on Jackson's door.

"Come in."

He was lying on his bed with his hands under his head. "Hey, Hartley, what's up?"

I had the metal box in my hands but didn't know what to say, so I just held it out. I guess, in the end, I really did just shove it at him.

"What's this?"

"Some cards. I didn't make them, somebody else did. But I collected them. I thought you might want them."

He took the box from me and I walked out of his room, along the hall, down the stairs, and out the front door.

It had become warm and humid, real summer weather. A black-and-orange cat I'd never seen before was stretched out on our walkway, looking at me. I crouched down to pat it and the cat started to purr.

I sat there for quite a while. And then the front door opened and Jackson came out. The cat stretched and padded away, almost as if it knew I didn't need its company anymore. Jackson was holding the metal box. He sat on the bottom step of the porch.

"These cards are really great."

"You think so?"

"Definitely. I mean, they gave me a lot to think about. I felt like I got to know the person who made them."

"Me too," I said.

"I think it's pretty special that you wanted to give them to me. But I think you should hold onto them."

"You want to give them back?"

"I just think they belong to you, Hartley. But I'd like to be able to look at them sometimes, if that's all right."

"Sure, it is."

"And together we could show them to Heather. I bet she would like them." Jackson held the box out for me to take.

"Okay."

"Thanks a lot, Hartley. And now I think I'm going to go for a walk."

"A walk? You're going to come back, right?"

"Definitely. I just like being on my own sometimes."

I watched him turn onto the sidewalk and walk down the street, his hands in his pockets. I watched until I couldn't see him anymore. Then I went upstairs and put the metal box in the desk drawer and came down again. And waited.

I waited an hour.

I waited until I saw Jackson appear at the end of the street, still with his hands in his pockets.

"Hey, Hartley."

"Hey, Jackson."

"Want to go inside? I'm hungry."

Now that he mentioned it, so was I. So the two of us went in and found my parents working side by side in the kitchen. George was sitting at the table looking at one of the *L'il Donkey* comics that used to be mine.

Heather came in through the back door. "I'm starving," she said.

"Well, who wants to help?" Mom asked.

"I will," Jackson said.

"Me too," Heather said.

"I'll help too," I added.

"Not me!" George laughed, leaning back his head.

"Oh, I've got a job for you too," Mom said. "Don't you worry about that. By the way, Hartley, there was a phone call for you."

"There was?"

"From Zack Mirani. He wanted to know if you would like to come over after dinner and shoot some hoops."

"Miss some hoops, you mean," Heather said.

"Oh, okay. I guess I will, then."

And so we made dinner, and put it on the table, and sat down together. Just like a regular family.

g.o.

The one color she hadn't yet used for a background was gold. In fact, she had avoided it. Too rich, too flashy, too optimistic.

But not today. She cut it out to match the size of the card and then glue-sticked it down. Then she went over to the typewriter and put in a sheet of paper.

what

i've realized

is

She kept typing, already knowing the words she wanted to say. They had been floating in her mind for a few days now. She typed the last word, pulled the sheet out of the typewriter, and went to the long worktable to cut them out.

And like the words, she already knew what she wanted for the images. This was going to be the most simple card of them all. That seemed appropriate for the last. It felt different this time, though, knowing that there was at least one person in the world who wanted to have it. She glued everything down and then added her initials and the card number.

Her dad called for her as she was coming down the hall. She found him in the kitchen, his wheelchair pulled up to the table, the Saturday paper spread out.

"I just made some herbal tea if you want some," he said.

"Sure."

She got herself a cup, poured from the old brown teapot, and sat across from him.

"So what's up with you?" he asked.

"Just another trip to the copy shop. Have you got an envelope?"

"There's some in the drawer under the toaster oven."

"Oh, right."

"You want to do something fun for dinner tonight? Maybe order pizza and watch a movie together? I'll even let you choose the movie."

"Sounds good, Dad." She got up and found an envelope and, taking a pen from the same drawer, came back to the table and wrote a name on it.

She looked at the name.

She took a breath.

"So Dad," she said, "there's something I wanted to tell you about."

"Sure." He folded the newspaper and pushed it away, looking up at her.

"It's about these girls at school."

"Friends?" her dad asked.

"No, definitely not friends. It's—well, it's a pretty big problem."

She felt tears in her eyes. She hadn't expected that. Her father reached out and took her hand.

"Tell me," he said.

29

Orange

For our summer holiday, we went on our usual camping trip. There was some trouble around whether Jackson would come or not. He wanted to stay home alone. After all, he said, he was almost seventeen. And he certainly knew how to take care of himself.

I guess my parents worried that he would leave again, or burn down the house, or not eat or shower or something. But in the end they agreed, on the conditions that Jackson checked in every day by phone and that he let Uncle Bill drop in.

We all missed having Jackson around, especially at night when we sat around the fire and told stories or jokes or sang corny songs. But knowing that he was okay allowed us to have a good time. Even Heather, who met some other kids her age, had a good time.

And when we came home, driving up in the car, tired from being on the road all day, there was Jackson sitting on the porch waiting for us. George was the first out of the car, running straight into Jackson's arms.

"Pew, do you smell!" Jackson said with a laugh.

Heather ran up to him next, whispering something into his ear, and then called out, "Dibs on the bathroom!" and ran into the house. That left me and my parents to unload the car, but Jackson helped.

I was taking in my last load, a couple of sleeping bags, when Jackson stopped me on the porch.

"Hey, Hartley," he said. "A letter came for you."

"A letter?"

"Hand-delivered. By a girl on a skateboard. With orange hair."

"Orange? I guess she must have changed it."

"Here, I'll take that stuff from you."

Jackson grabbed the sleeping bags and handed me the envelope. Then he went into the house, leaving me on the porch. I sat down on the step. The envelope had my name printed on it. I carefully tore it open and took out the card.

I looked at the card for a while, and then I noticed something else inside the envelope. A note. I took it out and read it.

what
i've realized
is

you
never
know
what
will
happen

next

g.o.

9

Hey,

Thought you might want this. I was kind of thinking
about you when I made it. I'm pretty sure it's the last
one. Time to move on to something new. Maybe you'll
make your own?

g.o.

I got up and went into the house, climbed the stairs, and closed the door of my room.

I took out the metal box and put all the cards on my desk. I had to do it in two rows.

Then I gathered them up again and put them in the metal box.

In my desk drawer I had a sheet of labels that my dad had given me. I peeled one off and stuck it to the top of the box. I used my best, neatest printing.

The Collected Works of Gretchen Oyster

I picked up the box and put it back in the drawer.

Opening my door, I realized something. I realized that I felt happy in a way that I hadn't for a long time.

Heather was coming out of the bathroom with one towel wrapped around her while she dried her hair with another.

"My turn!" I shouted.